KD

**No wonder he'd been so responsive to her touch!**

And her to his, of course. Between them they'd stacked up a lot of years of abstinence. Small surprise that their lovemaking had packed such a punch.

"I was more worried about getting pregnant," she explained. "I'm not on the Pill."

Again he went still, and then spoke, his voice flat and expressionless. "There's no need. When I said you're safe, I meant it in every sense. I can't get you pregnant, Anna."

Dear Reader,

I've heard it said a real writer has at least sixty books inside her. Well, I don't know about that, but I wrote my first book in 1990 and since then I've done fifty more. Maybe that makes me a real writer! Whatever, it isn't easy. Planning each book is like a pregnancy—painful and compelling. But the wow factor when the baby is born makes it all worthwhile!

Writing romances in a medical setting is a definite challenge—I have to keep up-to-date with what's going on in the medical world to be able to give enough detail to catch the reader's interest and give the setting authenticity. This gives me wonderful opportunities to develop the human-interest side of medicine, and I hope gives the books more depth and appeal.

*A Mother by Nature* was one that has been waiting in the wings. Anna, the heroine, has been "lurking" in several previous books until the right plot presented itself, and finally it came to me. My characters find their real strengths through the turmoil and tragedy that befalls them. I don't avoid reality, and I don't believe in fairy tales, but I do believe in the power of true love, and I hope you will, too, by the time you reach the end.

All the best,

Caroline

# A Mother by Nature

*Caroline Anderson*

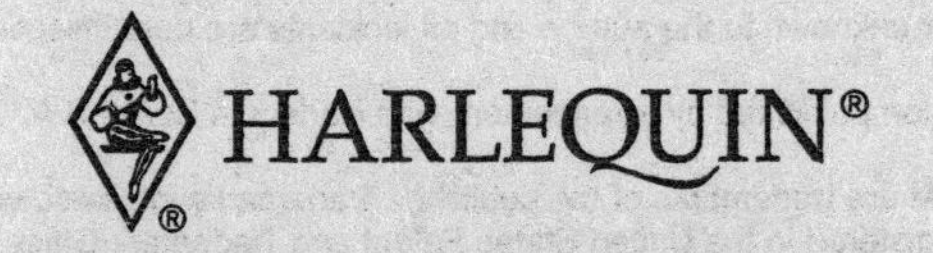


TORONTO • NEW YORK • LONDON
AMSTERDAM • PARIS • SYDNEY • HAMBURG
STOCKHOLM • ATHENS • TOKYO • MILAN • MADRID
PRAGUE • WARSAW • BUDAPEST • AUCKLAND

ISBN 0-373-06303-2

A MOTHER BY NATURE

First North American Publication 2001



This edition published by arrangement with Harlequin Books S.A.



Visit us at www.eHarlequin.com

**Printed in U.S.A.**

# CHAPTER ONE

HE STOOD in the bay window, his eyes scanning the dimly lit street with quiet contentment. It was a pleasant street, the large houses set back from the road and shielded from prying eyes by an avenue of old flowering cherries.

Their branches swayed in the wind, leafless still, the whispered promise of spring barely showing in the brave shoots of daffodils nudging the earth under the garden wall, but the signs were there, and he guessed it would be glorious when the trees blossomed.

A movement in the house opposite caught his attention, and he focused on it. There were lights on downstairs, and he could see people moving about, settling down for the evening.

His house was settled already, silent now except for the running footsteps on the stairs. They ground to a halt by the door.

'Adam? I'm going out now, OK?'

He looked towards the disembodied, slightly accented voice with resignation. 'OK. What time will you be back?' he asked, without any real hope that he would like the answer. He was right. He didn't.

'Late,' she said. 'I'm going to the pub again—maybe meet my new friends. I've got my keys.'

'OK. Goodnight, Helle.'

The front door slammed behind her, echoing through the house and making the windows rattle. Her feet crunched against the gravel of the drive, and she slipped through the gateway and disappeared, swallowed up by the eerie night. Adam dropped his head back against the edge of the window and let out a quiet sigh.

He was tired. It had been a hectic week. The move had taken three days, and he'd spent the next four unpacking and slotting things into their new places while the children had got under his feet and rushed about excitedly and Helle had done the bare minimum. The big Edwardian semi still seemed empty, the huge rooms swallowing up their meagre possessions with ease, but given time he could decorate all the rooms and buy more furniture to fill them.

It was a daunting thought, but there was no hurry, and just for now they were enjoying the novelty of having too much room. After nearly three years of battling for elbow room and falling over toys and clutter, it was wonderful to have the space to spread out.

Skye had her own bedroom for the first time, the boys' room was big enough to have a separate area for each of them, and Helle, their Danish au pair, had a room on the top floor, a huge room with a little shower off it next to the spare bedroom that would double as his study. That gave her privacy, and he had privacy and space of his own in the master bedroom suite at the front—most particularly space.

The size of his bedroom was the only incongruous thing. Like Helle's room above him, it ran across the full width of the front of the house, excluding the bathroom at the end, absurdly big compared to the middle bedroom he'd had at the other house and somehow highlighting his loneliness in a way which that cluttered little room had never done.

He dropped into a chair and closed his eyes, suddenly weary, and wondered how the children and Helle would cope without him tomorrow, his first day in his new job. How would he cope, come to that? It was not only a new job, but his first consultancy, and he felt a little rush of adrenaline at the thought. Nerves?

Absurd, Adam told himself. He was more than capable of doing it, more than ready for the responsibility and the challenge. It was just that with the move to a new area and a new house, a new school for Skye and Danny and a new nursery school for Jaz, there was so much change, so much to deal with.

Someone to share it with would have made it all so much easier, he thought with an inward sigh, but that hadn't been an option. And Helle had been more of a hindrance than a help since they'd moved. She'd been unhappy before, restless and discontented, and now, since they'd moved, she'd seemed permanently attached to the cordless phone, drifting aimlessly around and talking into it in Danish whenever she thought he wasn't listening. Phoning home? Lord alone knows what the phone bill will be, he thought grimly.

He had a feeling his au pair was destined for a fairly imminent departure, which would mean replacing her and settling the new girl in with the children while coping with the new job and trying to sort out the house.

That in itself would be no mean feat. They'd only been able to afford it because it needed to be grabbed by the scruff of the neck and dragged, kicking and screaming, into the next century. The plumbing was ancient and suspect, the heating was intermittent and unreliable, the wiring was safe but woefully inadequate, and there wasn't a single room that didn't need decorating and a new carpet and curtains.

Even on his new consultant's salary he couldn't afford to deal with it all at once, and he certainly couldn't afford to pay anyone to do it for him. Catapulting restlessly out of the chair, he went into the kitchen and poured himself a glass of wine. His eyes scanned the room without the benefit of his earlier rose-tinted spectacles, and the enormity of what he'd taken on swamped him.

It was the little things—the cupboard door that hung at a crazy angle because the top hinge had gone, the worktop that had a hole burned in it next to the cooker, the cracked and broken tiles, the broken sash cord that dangled from the window, taunting him.

How many others were on the point of breaking? What else was wrong that he hadn't noticed or worried about on the building society's huge and extensive survey report? OK, structurally it was sound, but everything he looked at seemed to need some attention. The loo off the hall needed to have its door rehung because it smashed into the basin behind it if you opened it more than halfway, the fireplace in the dining room needed to be opened up and revealed—the list was endless.

Endless, but cosmetic. Nothing time wouldn't cure. Once he'd had time to deal with it, it would be warm and light and a wonderful family home.

One day.

Adam went back to the drawing room, threw another shovel full of coal on the fire, put on a CD and settled down in the chair with his eyes firmly shut against the list of chores awaiting him in that room.

He didn't want to see the crack across the corner of the ceiling, the wallpaper easing off the wall just below it, the chipped paint on the skirting board, the worn and frayed carpet begging to be replaced.

There would be time for that later, once they were settled. In the meantime, he'd relax and try and get himself into the right frame of mind for tomorrow, and try not to think about Helle and the fact that she would probably disturb him coming back in the wee small hours of the night, doubtless utterly wasted after her evening in the pub, and would be hell to get up in the morning in time to get the children ready for school. Which meant he'd have to do it, yet again.

He put it out of his mind. He'd deal with tomorrow when it came. One day at a time, he reminded himself. It had got him through the last two years since Lyn had left. It would get him through the next twenty.

Please, God...

Damn. He was going to be late. His first day in his new job and he was going to be late.

'Daddy, I can't find my shoes...'

'Try under your coat on the floor in the dining room where you threw it last night. Jasper, eat your breakfast, please.'

'Don't like cornflakes.'

'You did yesterday. Danny, have you found your shoes yet?'

A mumble came from the dining room. It could just conceivably have been a yes. Then again...

Adam rammed his hands through his short, dark

hair and stared at the ceiling. Where was Helle? He'd called her three times.

'Do we have to go to school? I hate it there. I want to go back to my old school.'

Adam met Skye's sad blue eyes, old beyond her almost six years, and wished he could hug her and make her better. He'd given up trying. She simply stood and let him hold her, then walked away as soon as he let go. The social worker had said give her time, but it had been nearly three years now, and although she was better, she was still light years from emotional security.

And Lyn walking out on them hadn't helped one damn bit.

'Yes, darling, you do have to go,' he told her gently. 'You know that. I know it's hard at first, but you'll soon settle in and it'll be much better for us here near Grannie and Grandpa. You'll like seeing more of them, won't you?'

She shrugged noncommittally, and he stifled a sigh and went to the bottom of the stairs. 'Helle?' he yelled, and then remembered the neighbours through the party wall. Damn. At least the last house had been detached. Still, the people next door hadn't complained about their new neighbours yet, and the teenage girls had been round already to introduce themselves and offer their services for babysitting.

If Helle didn't get out of bed soon, he might have to take them up on it!

For what seemed like the millionth time, he wondered if he'd been quite mad to continue with the adoption when Lyn had left him. Maybe he should have let the kids go back instead of fighting to keep them. Maybe they would have been better off without him, with someone else instead. Two someones, preferably.

Then Danny wandered out into the hall, tie crooked, shoes untied, hair spiking on top of his head and a grin to gladden the loneliest heart, and he reached out and hugged the boy to his side as they went together back into the kitchen.

'Look—I made you a card at school.'

He handed Adam a crumpled bit of sugar paper with spider writing on it, pencil on dark grey, almost impossible to decipher and yet the message quite clear. 'I love you, Daddy. From Danny.' There was a picture stuck on the front, of a house with a wonky chimney and a red front door just like theirs. Swallowing hard to shift the lump in his throat, he thanked Danny and stuck the card on the front of the fridge with a magnet.

Skye, ever the mother, was coaxing Jasper to eat his now soggy cereal, and she looked up and gave Adam that steady, serious look that made him want to weep for her. 'Is Helle coming?' she asked, and he shook his head.

'I'm going to have to get her up,' he told them. 'I have to leave you guys and go to work, and I can't be late. Not today.'

'Are you scared?' Jasper asked, eyeing him curiously.

'Don't be stupid—course he's not!' Danny said patronisingly.

He sat down. 'Well, maybe a bit,' he confessed. 'Not scared exactly, but it's never easy to meet new people and settle into a new place. It doesn't matter if you're old or young, it's still a bit difficult at first.'

'Even for you?' Danny asked in amazement, gazing up at his hero with eyes like saucers.

He grinned and ruffled the spiky brown hair. 'Even for me, sport.'

'It'll be all right, you'll see,' Skye said seriously, neatly reversing their roles, and he felt a lump in his throat again.

No. Whatever chaos and drama they'd brought to his life, he couldn't imagine that life without them now. They belonged to each other, for better, for worse, and so on. They were a family and, like all families, they had good times and bad times.

Mostly they were good, but if Helle didn't get up soon, he had a feeling that today was going to be a bad one…

Anna was feeling blue. She'd woken that morning wondering what it was all about, and two hours later she was still no nearer the answer. Wake up, get up, eat, go to work, go home, eat, go to bed, wake up—relentless routine, day after day, with nothing to brighten it.

Was she just desperately ungrateful? She had a roof over her head—more than a roof, really, a lovely little house that she enjoyed and was proud of—great friends, and a wonderful job that she wouldn't change for the world—except that this morning, for the first time she could remember, she really, really didn't want to be here.

So what was the matter with her?

Stupid question. Anna knew perfectly well what was wrong with her. She was alone. She was twenty-eight years old, and she was alone, and she didn't want to be. She wanted to be married, and have children—lots of them—one after the other. Children of her own, not other people's little darlings but her own babies, conceived in love, nurtured by her body, raised by her and a man with dark hair and gentle eyes and a slow, sexy smile—a man she'd yet to meet.

Would never meet, she thought in frustration, if her life carried on as it was. Her biological clock was going to grind to a halt before then at this rate.

Oh, damn.

She pushed her chair back and stood up, her eyes automatically scanning the ward, and stopped dead as a jolt of recognition shot through her.

It was him. Dark hair, cut short but still long enough to have that sexy, unruly look that did funny things to her insides. Tallish, but not too tall, his shoulders broad enough to lean on but not wide enough to intimidate, he looked like a man you could rely on.

Her eyes scanned him, taking inventory. Lean hips. Firm chin and beautifully sculptured mouth. Eyebrows a dark slash across his forehead, mobile and expressive. A smile like quicksilver. He'd paused to chat to a child, his hands shoved deep into the pockets of his white coat, and the child was grinning and pointing towards her.

He was good-looking, certainly, but it wasn't really his looks that made him stand out so much as his presence. There was something about him, she thought as he straightened and turned towards her, something immensely strong and powerful and yet kind—endlessly, deeply kind, the sort of enduring kindness that made sacrifices and didn't count the cost.

She'd never seen him before, but her body recognised him, every cell on full alert.

He started towards her with a smile, and their eyes locked, and out of the blue, she thought, At last…!

'Sister Long?' he said, although he knew quite well who she was, if the badge on her tabard was to be believed.

'Anna,' she corrected, looking up at him with startling green eyes, and he felt a shiver of sexual awareness which had lain dormant for so long it was almost shocking. A wisp of dark red hair had escaped from her neat bob and was falling forward over her face, and he had to restrain himself from lifting it with his fingers and tucking it back behind her ear. She smiled and held out her hand, slim and firm and purposeful. 'You must be our new paediatric orthopaedic consultant—Mr Bradbury, isn't it?'

He nodded. 'Adam,' he said, and his voice cracked and he cleared his throat. 'Adam Bradbury. Good to meet you. Have you got time for a chat? My department seem to have organised things so that I'm at a total loose end today, so I thought I'd spend it orienteering.'

She chuckled, a low, sexy chuckle that made his hair stand on end and everything else jump to attention. 'Sure. Come into the kitchen, I'll make coffee.'

He followed her, his eyes involuntarily tracking over the neat waist, the gentle swell of her hips, the womanly sway as she pushed the door out of the way and turned to hold it for him, flashing him a smile with those incredibly expressive eyes.

She spoke, but his body was clamouring so loud he didn't hear her.

'I'm sorry?'

She gave him a quizzical smile. 'I said, tea or coffee?'

'Oh—tea, thank you,' he said, trying to concentrate on something other than her warm, soft mouth. 'It's a bit early for coffee.'

'Well, there's a thing. A fellow tea-drinker. Everyone else dives straight for the coffee.' The smiled softened, lighting up her changeable green eyes and bringing out the gold flecks.

Not green at all, he realised, but blue and gold, fascinating eyes, beautiful eyes.

Bedroom eyes.

Oh, lord.

He stuffed his hands back into his coat pockets and angled them across his body as a shield. He had to work with her. He really, really didn't need the embarrassment of an adolescent reaction!

Anna took him on a guided tour while the kettle boiled. She was glad to get out of the tiny kitchen, to be honest, the current running between them seemed so powerful. Not that he'd really given her any hint that he was interested, but there just seemed to be something that hummed along under the surface.

'We've got twenty-one beds,' she told Adam, walking down the ward towards the orthopaedic section, his area of special interest. 'Six acute medical, six surgical, six orthopaedic and three single or family suites for more critical or noisy or infectious patients. We've got an isolation ward for barrier nursing or immuno-compromised patients—that's another single, but I don't tend to count it. It's the only room that doesn't get stolen for other things.'

'Stolen?' he said with a slow smile.

Anna rolled her eyes. 'Oh, yes, of course—the lines

get blurred and we end up with kids muddled up in the wrong place because of numbers, which drives the bed manager potty and the consultants come to blows over who has which bed for which child.'

His mouth kicked up in a crooked smile of appreciation, and her heart flip-flopped in her chest. Concentrate, she told herself sternly.

'We keep the age groups together if we can—the long-stay older kids are the worst, as you might imagine, and the teenagers in traction are a nightmare.'

'Well, there's a thing,' he murmured. 'You could always put any really difficult kids in the Stryker bed for a little while just to get a taste of real deprivation of liberty.'

'What, like throwing prisoners of war into the cooler? What a fascinating thought...!'

He laughed, and she thought her knees were going to give way. He's probably married with a million children, she chided herself crossly, and told herself to mind her own business.

'Have you moved far?' she asked as they walked down the ward, her insatiable curiosity getting the better of her anyway.

'About a hundred and fifty miles or so. I was in Oxford.'

'Oxford? How lovely. How will you cope with the rural isolation of Audley?' she asked with a laugh, and then her mouth, running on without her permission, added, 'Doesn't your wife mind?'

'She might if I had one, but I don't,' Adam said lightly.

'That must make it easier,' she replied, trying not to smile with delight because he was free, but his next words took the wind right out of her sails.

'Not really,' he told her. 'I've got three children under six and a Danish au pair with attitude, and we've bought a huge Edwardian house that needs every nook and cranny kicked into shape. Easier it's not, but I like a challenge.'

She ground to a halt outside the playroom, and turned towards him, guilt prickling her. 'I'm sorry,' she said sincerely. 'I didn't mean to intrude.'

'You're not intruding,' he said with a gentle smile that reassured her slightly. 'I'm just feeling a little overawed by what I've taken on. How about you? Are you married? Single, widowed, divorced, or other, please specify?'

Anna laughed, relief flooding through her at his light-hearted tone. 'Single,' she replied. Endlessly. Regrettably.

She never found out what he would have said next, because the playroom door flew open and a child came barrelling through it full pelt and nearly knocked her over. Her hand flew out and grabbed him by the shoulder, steadying him, and she looked down into his sparkling, mischievous eyes and shook her head.

'You'll never learn, Karl, will you?'

He grinned. 'Sorry, Sister. I was in a hurry.'

'I noticed. That was how this happened in the first place, wasn't it? Too much of a hurry?' She eyed him thoughtfully. 'You're going to hurt someone with that cast in a minute as well. Do me a favour and go and sit down and do something quiet. You'll be going up to Theatre later this morning, and you really could do with being calm beforehand.'

'Perhaps Karl should be our first experiment with the Stryker bed?' Adam said softly under his breath.

'What a good idea,' Anna murmured, eyeing young Karl thoughtfully.

He looked from one to the other, not sure what they were talking about but obviously edgy. 'What's a—whatever you said sort of bed?' he asked suspiciously.

'You lie in it like the filling in a sandwich, and it turns over from time to time. It's for keeping people with certain conditions like spinal injuries very still.'

'Or settling down overactive youngsters,' Adam added with a smile that belied his words.

'You're winding me up,' Karl said, still not quite sure, and Anna laughed and ruffled his hair.

'You got it. Go and find something quiet to do, there's a good lad, and I'll come and give you your pre-med later.'

He shot off, clearly relieved, and with a smile they headed back towards the kitchen. 'He's got a non-union of the radius after a nasty fracture. They just can't get it to heal, so they're going to sort him out in Theatre this morning and probably pack it and plate it. I'm not sure if they've decided exactly what they're doing.'

'Who's doing it?' he asked.

'Robert Ryder. Have you met him yet?'

Adam shook his head. 'No. Perhaps I'll track him down, see if I can observe. Might be interesting.'

'I'm sure he won't mind, he's very approachable. How about that tea now?' she added as they arrived back at the nursing station by her office. But then the phone rang and it was A and E to say that there was a patient on the way up, a frequent visitor who had suffered yet another serious asthma attack and was now stable but needing observation.

'Can you hang on?' she asked him, explaining the

case briefly to him. 'I really need to see to this child, he's a regular. Or you could help yourself to tea. You're more than welcome.'

'I'll pass. I'll go and meet the rest of the paediatric team about the hospital, and make a nuisance of myself elsewhere. I might go into the orthopaedic theatres and have a nose around, introduce myself to Ryder and see if I can observe Karl's op, as I said.'

She felt a pang of what could only have been regret. 'OK. Maybe next time,' she suggested, and could have kicked herself for sounding like a breathless virgin. Ridiculous. She was too busy to have tea with him anyway! 'Have a good day,' she added with a smile.

'I'm sure I will—and thanks for the guided tour. I'll see you tomorrow, no doubt.'

Anna watched him go out of the corner of her eye as she scanned the ward for the most suitable place to put young Toby Cardew, and she suddenly realised that she was looking forward to the next day for the first time in ages.

Gone were the blues she'd felt that morning, replaced by a shiver of anticipation. Adam was apparently unencumbered by a wife, the fact that he had children already was hardly a turn-off to a paediatric nurse and, anyway, the more the merrier.

You're getting ahead of yourself, she cautioned as she went to sort out a bed for Toby. Just because you think he's attractive and he asked about your marital status, that doesn't mean it will go any further—and, anyway, he might have terrible habits. Why did his wife leave him?

*She might have died. Perhaps he's suffering from intractable grief,* her alter ego suggested.

Funny. He didn't look like a man suffering from intractable grief. He just looked tired round the eyes, and, if she hadn't been mistaken, he'd been interested in her. She hadn't been mistaken. She knew that look. She'd had plenty of practice at intercepting it over the years.

Too many years, too many times, too many near-misses. The trouble was, the older she got the more likely that the men of her age would be already settled in a permanent relationship—at least, the ones worth having!

Maybe this was one time when she wouldn't have to fend the man off. Maybe this time the advances, when and if they came, would be welcome. Goodness knows, it's about time, she thought.

'Who was *that*?'

Anna looked round at Allie Baker, her staff nurse and second in command, and wagged a finger.

'You've got one of your own,' she told her friend.

Allie grinned. 'I know, and I wouldn't swap him for the world. I just thought whoever that was was rather gorgeous. So who is he?'

'Adam Bradbury, our new paediatric orthopaedic surgeon.'

'I didn't know we had an old one.'

'We haven't,' Anna replied with a smile, checking forms on the clipboard at the end of the vacant bed. 'It's a new post. He's going to be doing developmental problems and post-traumatic reconstruction, that sort of thing, as well as working with the oncologists on bone cancers and the neurologists on spina bifida and so on. I gather he's rather clever.'

Allie grinned. 'And he's got your name on him.'

Anna smiled self-consciously. 'I don't know. I hope so. He's got three kids and no wife.'

'Oh, my God.' Allie looked at her in horror. *'Three kids?'*

Anna shrugged. 'I like kids.'

'You'd have to, working with them all day and going home to them at night. Maybe they're teenagers and nearly off his hands. Maybe they live some of the time with his wife.'

Anna laughed and pushed Allie out of the way gently. 'I'll tell you if I ever get a chance to find out. In the meantime, I've got things to do and you're holding me up. Toby Cardew's coming back.'

Allie rolled her eyes. 'Not again? Whatever this time?'

'I have no idea. This attack was quite severe, I gather. His parents are going potty trying to find the trigger. Their house must be so clean! Mrs Cardew spends hours a day mopping it down.'

'Maybe it's not the house. Maybe it's school, or something on the journey, or a kid he sits next to?'

'They've addressed all that. Maybe one day it will fall into place—it's probably something really obvious that they've overlooked.'

The squeak of the A and E trolley alerted them to the new arrival, and Anna went to greet him. 'Hello again, young man,' she said with a smile of welcome, and patted his hand reassuringly. 'Can't stay away, can you? Must be our wit and charm that keeps you coming back.'

The boy gave a weak grin, and his mother shot Anna a tired, slightly desperate smile. 'Sorry to be a nuisance,' she apologised, but Anna brushed her words aside.

'Don't be silly,' she said briskly. 'That's why we're here, and we're always pleased to see a familiar face. Right, let's have you in bed and make you comfortable, shall we?'

They quickly shifted young Toby across onto the bed and settled him, then left him to rest. Allie made Mrs Cardew a cup of coffee, Anna went to give Karl his pre-med and it only seemed like five minutes before the boy was back from Theatre, his arm cast in a back slab to allow for swelling and with the hand raised.

He wouldn't be running around for a few days at least, Anna thought, and wondered if Adam *had* observed the operation. No doubt she'd find out tomorrow.

A tiny surge of what felt like adrenaline ran through her, and she caught herself looking at her watch and counting the hours until she'd see him again...

## CHAPTER TWO

ADAM was due to start the day with a clinic, followed by a ward round to meet the new admissions on whom he'd operate that afternoon. He'd gone back to the ward and checked the notes yesterday evening, and had been foolishly disappointed to find that Anna had gone.

Pity. He'd wanted to tell her about his part in Karl's operation, and discuss what they'd done.

Strictly business, of course. Still, he'd see her today.

That lock of hair that kept falling forward and curving round her cheek was plaguing him. He'd been having fantasies about it all night—which was crazy because he always had fantasies about dark hair spread across his pillow in a fan, and hers was short and red. Dark red, admittedly, but red for all that, and far too short to fan satisfactorily.

Still, he wondered how it would feel sifting through his fingers…

Like silk. It was soft, heavy hair, essentially straight, with just enough bounce to curve under and curl around the pale pearly shell of her ear…

Damn.

He scooped the post off the floor in the lobby and scanned through it, grinding to a halt at the telephone bill. It was the final bill for the old house, and it took his mind off Anna and her attributes very effectively.

He opened it with grim resignation, but even his

wildest expectations were exceeded by its stunning proportions. Helle must truly have spent all day, every day, on the phone to her family and friends in Denmark.

He shook his head in despair, and ran upstairs to her room, rapping loudly on the door. 'Helle? Get up now. I want to talk to you immediately.'

There was a shuffling noise, and the door opened to reveal his hapless young au pair, her hair on end, her eyes blurred with sleep, dragging on a dressing-gown.

'What's the matter?' she asked, looking puzzled.

'This is the matter,' Adam said tightly, brandishing the thing under her nose. 'The telephone bill. It runs into four figures, Helle, and it's not even a complete quarter. I want you downstairs dressed in five minutes, and you'd better have a damn good explanation or you'll be packing your bags and catching the next flight home.'

'Good,' she said miserably, and burst into tears. 'I want to go home. I hate it here.'

You're a sucker, he told himself as he opened his arms and comforted the young woman while she cried. She was little more than a child herself, and it was a lot of responsibility. He should have talked to her more, been kinder to her, instead of expecting so much.

'Come downstairs,' he said more gently, easing her out of his arms. 'We'll have a cup of tea and talk about it before the children get up.'

She nodded and sniffed, scrubbing her nose on the sleeve of her dressing-gown. 'I'll get dressed.'

'Good idea.'

He ran back down, put the kettle on and glanced

at his watch. It was still only six-thirty, and he wondered if Anna was up yet or if she worked nine to five to cover admissions and pre- and post-ops. If she worked shifts and was on an early she'd be on her way there now. If not, she might still be in bed, her hair tangled round her face, her lashes like crescents on her cheeks, her mouth soft with sleep—

'You need a life, Bradbury,' he growled, and banged two mugs down on the worktop just as Helle came into the room.

She hovered apprehensively in the doorway, and he waved her in. 'Come in, sit down, I'm not going to bite you. I just want to know what's going on.'

She sat but, being Helle, she couldn't just sit. She played with the salt, she shredded a paper towel that had been left on the table, tearing it systematically into tiny strips while she waited for the axe to fall.

'Talk to me. Tell me all about it,' Adam said softly, sliding a mug across the battered old pine table, and she looked up, her eyes like huge pools filling yet again.

'I'm just lonely—I want my mum. I'm homesick. I thought it would get better, but then you said we were moving and I had to say goodbye to all my friends, and I thought, how will I cope in a new place?'

A tear fell, splashing on her hand, and she scrubbed it away and went on, 'It was hard before, when my friend Silke was just round the corner. Now it's impossible. I don't know anybody, and the children are at school and there's nothing to do, and I just sit and cry—'

'So you ring your mum.'

She nodded miserably. 'I'm sorry, Adam. I didn't realise it would be so expensive.'

'It's as much as your wages,' he pointed out, not unreasonably.

'But some is you,' she defended with truth, and he shrugged.

'A little. Perhaps the first hundred pounds.'

She swallowed. 'May I see it?'

He handed her the bill—the itemised section that ran to page after page—and she studied it in silence and handed it back.

'Are you going to send me home?'

'Do you want to go? Do you really want to go? Are you so unhappy? I don't want you to be unhappy, Helle. It doesn't help anyone—not you, not me, and certainly not the children.'

She nodded and sniffed. 'I do want to go. I'll miss the children, but I'm so lonely. It wouldn't be so bad if you had a wife, it would be another woman to talk to. It's different—I can't talk to you like I could to a woman.'

Nothing would be so bad if he had a wife, he thought defeatedly, including his own loneliness, but it was out of the question. Lyn's defection had scarred them all, and there was no way he was going there again.

'I'll ask my mum,' Helle went on, miserably shredding another paper towel. 'Maybe she'll pay the phone bill.'

'Never mind the phone bill. Just do me a favour and stay until I can get someone else, and then I'll forget the bill—OK? Only stay off the damn phone in the daytime, please, until you go home. Deal?'

He wouldn't understand women if he lived to be a

hundred, he thought as Helle burst into tears. He found her an unshredded piece of kitchen roll and watched as she hiccuped to a halt and blotted herself up.

'Deal,' she said finally.

'Good. Now, do you suppose you could get the children up in time for school today, please?'

She nodded. 'I'll wake them now.'

He ate a piece of toast, kissed the children hello and goodbye in one and left for work, his mind on his afternoon list. He had yet to meet the other members of his firm, the registrars and house doctors that were allocated to him in this new speciality that the Audley Memorial had set up.

Most hospitals had one or two consultants who tended to handle the paediatric work. It was unusual to find a post dedicated to it, and he was looking forward to the challenge. He understood they would take referrals from other hospitals within the region once his post was established—it would become the local specialist centre for paediatric orthopaedics, centralising treatment in Suffolk and making it more accessible for patients and their families.

That meant better visiting arrangements, which in turn meant happier patients getting better quicker. He approved of that.

Adam parked his car in the staff car park, then crossed it and palmed the door out of the way and caught himself all but running down the corridor to the ward. Idiot, he thought crossly. She's probably not even there yet—and if she is, she'll be busy.

She was. She was taking report, and he went into the kitchen and put the kettle on and made two mugs of tea. She wouldn't be long.

* * *

'Tea,' he said, thrusting a mug at her, and Anna took it gratefully and drank it too fast, almost scalding her mouth. It was delicious—almost as delicious as him—and nearly as welcome.

'I needed that. How did you know?' she said with a smile as she drained it, and he gave a chuckle and made her another one.

'I wanted to go through the notes of my afternoon list with you,' he said over his shoulder as he stirred the teabag round. 'I think you know some of the patients.'

She nodded. 'Sure. Shall we go into the office?'

'Have you got time?'

She grinned at him. 'One of the nice things about this job is being able to delegate most of it! Come on, I can spare you ten minutes. The notes are in there still.'

She settled down in her chair, her knees propped up on the edge of the desk, her uniform trousers protecting her modesty. 'Tell me about Karl first,' she prompted, trying to concentrate on something other than his long, lean legs stretched out across the floor in her office and the casual way he slouched against her desk.

'Karl? Oh, the lad yesterday. Robert let me assist—it was interesting. We plated it. When we got in there it was quite obvious that the bone had made no attempt to heal. The main reason seemed to be that it had rotated out of alignment, so we had to break the ulna as well to correct the rotation so we could line it all up properly. We plated both just to be on the safe side. It should be a better shape than it was before, anyway, so in a strange way it might have done him a favour. How is he now?'

'Bit groggy. Quieter than yesterday, I gather. I think he had quite a good night. Was it very traumatic to the tissues?'

He shrugged. 'Fairly. I would expect it to be quite sore for a day or two. It was obviously quite a nasty break—I had a look at the earlier plates. It seems likely that he tried to do too much too soon and twisted it out of position inside the cast. By the time it was noticed, it was too late.'

'That's what you get for trying to fix an active young hellion conservatively,' Anna said with a smile. 'They need everything screwed together because they all want a quick fix.'

'Everybody wants a quick fix,' he said with a sigh. 'I think my au pair's going to want a quick fix. I confronted her with the phone bill this morning and she announced she wanted to go home. I bribed her by offering to forget the phone bill if she'd stay until I'd got a replacement.'

'And?'

He shrugged. 'She says she'll stay—for now, at least.'

Anna felt a pang of sympathy. 'Was it horrendous?' she asked, and he rolled his eyes.

'Try four figures.'

Anna's jaw dropped. For the life of her she couldn't conceive of finding time to build up a phone bill that huge, never mind having anyone she wanted to talk to that much!

Well. Maybe that wasn't true—not any more. She could imagine curling up in the evening and having long, cosy chats to this man—

'Let's talk about your afternoon list,' she said,

dragging herself back to earth hastily. 'Who have you got that I know?'

'A baby with congenital club foot? David Chisholm. I think he's been in here. He's about eighteen months.'

Anna thought for a moment. 'David—yes, he has. I remember him. He's had a couple of ops already to let out the short structures on the inside of the legs. He was very bad—worst case I've seen, I think, not that we've had that many. I thought they'd got quite a good result?'

Adam nodded. 'That's right, but he needs another op because he's grown and the feet are turning in again.'

'Aren't they splinting it?'

He nodded again. 'Yes, but it's not keeping up. I'm going to release the tendons again—it's fairly rare, of course, so you don't tend to get that much practice at this sort of thing, but we're learning new ways of dealing with it. Sadly, it's never going to be quite normal, of course, and I haven't met the parents yet so I don't know what their expectations are.'

'High, I think. Most parents' expectations are high. They think we can sort out everything.'

'Well, I'll certainly try my best, but I'm only human,' he said with a wry smile, and her heart hiccuped. Only human's fine by me, she wanted to tell him, but she was being silly again.

One smile! she thought crossly. One smile and you keel over and submit! You'd make a good dog.

Anna tried to pay attention—she really did—but it was hard. In the end she was rescued by the arrival of a new admission, and she went to deal with him and escaped from the intoxicating and mind-bending cosiness of her office. She was busy for the rest of the day, rushed off her feet for most of it, and by the end of it she was feeling ragged.

Then Adam walked onto the ward, still in Theatre scrubs, and her heart did that silly thing all over again and she wanted to kick herself.

'Hi,' he said, his voice soft and low. Shivers ran down her back, and she forced herself to ignore them.

'Hi, yourself,' she said with what she hoped was a friendly smile and not an infatuated drool. 'How was your list?'

'OK. A couple are in SCBU, but you should have the rest. How's little David?'

'Sick and sore, I think. Well, probably more uncomfortable than sore. His mother's with him, but she's pregnant again and she's finding it quite wearing. I keep sending my nurses to rescue her so she can go and have a cup of tea, but she won't let me.'

'Is she staying all night?'

Anna nodded. 'Yes. She needs to rest, but she won't leave him till he settles.'

'Can I have a quick look?' he asked.

'Sure. He's over here.'

They went over to the baby and his mother and, as Anna had expected, the little boy was propped up against her shoulder, grizzling gently, and she was rubbing his back and making soothing noises. They weren't working.

'Hello, Mrs Chisholm,' Adam said, hunkering down to her level and smiling at her with that special smile. 'How are things?'

'Oh—hello, Doctor. I'm so glad you've come. Not too bad. How was it? Have you been able to do it?'

'It was OK,' he said reassuringly. 'I've managed

to get quite a bit of length on the tendons, so we were able to get his feet into a more normal position in the casts. He'll be a bit miserable for a day or so, but we're giving him plenty of pain relief so he's not really hurting. Once the first few days are over you'll find he's walking much better. May I have a look?'

She held the little boy out, and Adam took him and straightened.

'Hello again, young man. Can I have a look at your feet?' he said softly, his smile gentle. The baby rested sleepily against him with a little whimper, and Adam soothed him automatically before laying him down in the cot.

His movements were sure and practised, Anna thought. You could tell he was a father. His hand brushed the baby's head, smoothing back the damp, ruffled hair that clung to his brow, and quickly he scanned the boy's legs with his eyes.

'I'm checking the colour and warmth of his toes and that the dressings you can see through these windows in the casts aren't showing signs of leaking of the wounds,' he explained. 'Perhaps you could keep an eye on that for us, as you're here. It's possible the legs might swell after a little while, but we'll keep a constant check, and if you notice anything different, perhaps you could tell us.'

She nodded. 'Of course.'

'He looks fine at the moment,' he went on, raising his voice over the baby's unhappy protests. 'I'm pleased. He seems a bit grizzly, though. Perhaps he's not that comfortable. We'll give him something to settle him.'

'I think he needs to sleep,' Mrs Chisholm said, 'but

every time I put him down he cries, and I don't like to disturb the other children.'

'Don't worry about the other children,' Anna hastened to assure her. 'He won't cry for long. He's dead beat. He'll go off in seconds if you can just bear to let him cry.'

'I just feel so mean,' she said, clearly torn.

'Perhaps you should go and get something to eat and leave him quietly alone for a little while and try it,' Adam suggested. 'You might find he drops off if you aren't here to cuddle—it's not worth staying awake then.' The smile robbed his suggestion of any criticism, and she nodded wearily.

'I could murder a cup of tea and a leg stretch, and probably something to eat, actually. I was going to wait until my husband came back and go then, so David wasn't on his own, but are you sure he'll be all right?'

'Of course he'll be all right,' Anna assured her firmly. 'We'll look after him. If he doesn't settle in a minute I'll get someone to cuddle him till you're back, but you've got to look after yourself and the other baby.'

She nodded again. 'OK. Thanks.'

They watched her go, and she was hardly out of the ward before little David stopped grizzling and started to relax into much-needed sleep.

'Peace at last,' Anna said with a soft chuckle, and covered the little boy lightly with his blanket. 'He'll be all right now. Do you still want to give him something?'

Adam shook his head. 'Not if he doesn't need it. I'll write him up for something in case he wakes in the night and is distressed. What are you doing now? Got time to look at my others with me?'

She glanced at the clock on the wall and groaned. 'Not really. Apparently, it's time to go home and I still haven't finished. Do you need me with you to look at your other patients?'

'I wouldn't mind, but it isn't necessary. Anyway I suspect they're all asleep. Are their parents here?'

'Yes, all of them. I'm sure they'd love to see you and ask you about the operations.'

He nodded, pursed his lips for a moment as he, too, glanced at his watch, and then he shrugged. 'I'll go and see them. You don't have to stay, I'm sure I can find my way around.'

'I'll show you where they are and leave you to it. I have to hand over to Allie. Those two beds there,' she told him, pointing, 'and that one in the far corner. OK? Shout if you need help. Allie will sort you out.'

'OK. Thanks. See you tomorrow.'

His smile warmed her. Reluctantly, she dragged herself back to her other tasks, handed over and left the ward with only a handful of backward glances.

She went home, put the kettle on while she changed into jeans and a comfy sweater, and sat down with her feet up and a cup of tea in front of the TV news. It didn't hold her attention. It couldn't even begin to compete with that sexy smile and the smoky green eyes that were beginning to haunt her every waking moment.

What made him so different? Nothing obvious. Over the years she'd been out with several men, most of them very pleasant, most of them perfectly nice.

Nice. Pleasant.

She didn't *want* 'nice' and 'pleasant'. She wanted

someone who made her blood sing, whose touch would reduce her to putty, whose eyes could turn her heart inside out and melt her into a puddle at his feet.

They hadn't all been nice, of course. There had been Jim—he'd been charming and utterly faithless. She'd had her fingers burned by him and had been much more circumspect after that. Not that she'd ever been in the slightest bit promiscuous, but everyone seemed to imagine that if you dated them more than twice at the outside you were destined for bed.

Anna didn't work like that. It had to be right, and it had only been right very rarely. Just recently—like in the last three years or so—it hadn't been right at all.

'You're turning into a desperate old maid,' she said in disgust. 'One smile from a halfway presentable man and you're there waiting with your tongue hanging out. That's so sad.'

She smacked her mug down, stood up and went through into the kitchen. The fridge revealed very little of any interest, and the freezer was worse.

'Great,' she said in disgust. 'I have to go shopping. Marvellous.'

She slammed the freezer door, stuffed her feet into her old trainers and pulled on her tatty but snuggly duffle-coat. She wasn't going to see anyone. She didn't need to dress up.

She drove to the nearest supermarket, picked up a little trolley and started wandering randomly up and down the aisles. Nothing appealed. Well, nothing healthy. She glanced into the trolley next to her, wondering what other people ate that might be more interesting than the usual things that she bought, and she sighed.

Fish fingers, low-fat oven chips, frozen veg, chicken legs, rice—about as inspired as hers, except that this trolley actually had something in it.

Three loaves of bread, lots of tuna and ham and salad ingredients, little cakes—lots of convenience foods, really, she thought. Busy household. Working mother, probably. Poor woman—

'Anna?'

She looked up, startled, and found Adam looking at her curiously.

'Hi,' she said weakly.

'Hi. Thought it was you. Is there something wrong with my trolley?'

'Your— No, of course not! I didn't know it was yours. I was looking in it for inspiration, actually.'

He gave a wry snort of laughter. 'I should give it a miss, in that case. I buy what the kids will eat, which sometimes seems like utter rubbish. It's the au pair's job, of course, but she's having the evening off, so it's down to me to buy the junk food today.'

'It doesn't look too bad. At least you're going for the low-fat options.'

'Ever the conscientious father,' he said with a fleeting smile. 'Which reminds me, they're running riot in the next aisle. I must go.'

She watched him disappear round the end of the aisle and, because she was only human and curiosity was part of human nature, she found herself drifting after him. They'd vanished, but she soon found them.

He was lifting a little boy off the top of the bread display unit, smiling apologetically at a disapproving member of staff and throwing a packet into the trolley with one hand while he clamped the protesting child to his side with the other.

'No, if you can't behave then you'll have to stay here with me where I can keep an eye on you.'

'I'll look after him,' a little girl promised, and Adam put the boy down. 'Stay right next to me,' she told him sternly, and he nodded and slipped his hand into hers.

Big sister, Anna thought with a gentle smile.

'Daddy, can we have supper here, please?'

The middle one, Anna thought, looking at the little face shining up at him with obvious devotion. What a lovely family. A huge lump formed in her throat, and she was just about to slide round the corner of the aisle and find a little privacy to get herself under control when Adam turned and saw her.

'Um—yes, sure,' he said distractedly, and smiled at her. She wondered if he knew he'd just been conned, and had to hide her own smile of amusement behind a smile of greeting. 'My brood,' he said, waving at them. 'Skye, Danny, Jasper, this is Miss Long. I work with her.'

'Anna,' she corrected, and directed her smile to the children. 'Hi. Are you making sure he buys all the right things?'

'No, they're making sure I buy all the *wrong* things,' he said with a laugh.

'We're going to have supper here,' Danny told her. 'Do you ever do that?'

'I have done,' she said, willing Adam to ask her to join them. He didn't need to. Danny did it.

'You could have supper with us—couldn't she, Daddy?' He swivelled his head round, leaning over backwards and nearly toppling into the bread.

Adam reached out and steadied him, and gave Anna a helpless look. 'If you'd like to—you're more than welcome to join us, if you can stand it. It'll probably be egg, beans and chips if they get their way.'

Thank you, God! 'Egg, beans and chips sounds good,' she said with a bright smile. 'If you mean it.'

'Of course I mean it,' he said, his eyes softening. 'You're more than welcome. Are you all done?'

'Yes,' she lied. To hell with doing the shopping. She'd get the rest another time. This was much more interesting!

They went through the checkout, parked their trolleys and joined the queue, and Danny chatted ingenuously all the way through the selection procedure and most of the way through the meal. He was a sweet, open child with spiky, untidy hair the same dark brown as his father's, and a direct blue gaze that cut straight to her heart.

Jasper was similar—smaller and quieter, or perhaps simply overwhelmed by his big brother, hanging on his sister's every word.

And Skye—Skye was different. She had soft, lustrous brown hair, not quite as dark as the others, and the same penetrating blue eyes, but there the similarities ended.

Her eyes were distrustful. That was the difference, Anna decided. Skye was guarded, she hardly spoke except to Jaz, and she was politely distant with Anna.

That was fine. She didn't need the instant trust of every child in the world, but she sensed that Skye's reticence hurt Adam, and for some reason she didn't want to go into that hurt her, too.

There was only one awkward moment, when she wondered if she really ought to have been there. Skye looked at Adam and said softly, 'Is Anna your girlfriend?'

He looked startled for a second, then shook his head. 'No. We work together. She's a nurse.'

Skye glanced at her consideringly, then went back to her meal without another word, leaving Anna thoughtful. It hadn't sounded, from her tone of voice, as if a girlfriend was something Skye wanted Adam to have. Because she felt threatened? Because she was jealous? Or because he had a constant stream of them and Skye didn't like it?

The table was crowded, and Anna was more than ever aware of Adam's long legs tangling with hers every time he moved. Finally the children were finished, and he met her eyes over the litter of dirty plates and cups of fizzy drinks and smiled distractedly.

'We have to get back. We've got frozen food in the trolley—or we did have. I expect it's all thawed by now.'

She nodded, conscious of a silly little spurt of disappointment. Of course he had to go—Jasper was yawning, Skye was bored and uneasy, and they couldn't possibly sit there all night. She conjured a bright smile. 'Yes, you'd better get back. Thank you so much for asking me to join you. I enjoyed it.'

He gave a disbelieving snort of laughter. 'You're too polite. Come on, kids, on your pins, let's make a move.'

She followed him out of the shop, looking like the Pied Piper with the children trailing behind him raggedly. Jasper kept wanting to look at things, and had to be dragged screaming past the little rocket ride just outside the door, with its coaxing invitation, 'Come on, climb aboard and we'll head for the skies!'

'I want to have a go!' Jasper sobbed, and Adam

scooped him up into his arms and hugged him, walking resolutely away.

'It's too late. You can have a go next time. It's too cold to hang about waiting, and we can't do everything in one night.'

'Don't want to do everything! Want to go in the rocket!'

'Jasper, Daddy said no,' Skye told him firmly, and the screaming subsided to an unhappy sobbing. They paused at the edge of the car park, and Adam rolled his eyes at Anna in mock despair.

'I'll see you tomorrow,' she said, and he nodded, hesitated a moment and then spoke as if on impulse.

'You could come back for coffee—if you could stand the chaos of bedtime and a house that needs cleaning and decorating from attic to cellar.'

A slow smile spread over her face. She could stand anything if it meant spending time with him and his family and getting to know him better. 'I should think I'll cope with that,' she said softly.

'Follow me,' he said.

Oh, yes, she thought. I'll follow you. I'll follow you to the ends of the earth if you ask me to. Just say the word.

Then she caught the look on Skye's face, and wondered why the little girl was so unhappy about her presence. She needed to know more about the situation, and perhaps this was one way to find out.

# CHAPTER THREE

'OH, IT'S gorgeous!'

Adam looked mildly disbelieving, but Anna shook her head at him and laughed, gazing around, enraptured, at the lovely, welcoming hallway with its high ceilings and gleaming mahogany handrail. 'It is! It's truly wonderful—oh, it's going to be so lovely. It just feels—I don't know, *right.*'

'That's what I felt. It's why I bought it,' Adam said with a smile, but then the smile grew wry. 'Emphasis on "going to be", though. If and when I ever get the time and the money—not to mention the energy. Right, kids, upstairs and get yourselves ready for bed, please. It's way past your bedtime. I'll be up in five minutes.'

They ran up, and Adam seized several of the shopping bags from the hall floor and headed towards the back of the house. Anna picked up a couple more and followed him.

'You'll do it—don't be so defeatist. It's early days—heavens, most people wouldn't even have unpacked yet!'

'I haven't, not entirely. The dining room's still stacked up with boxes, but they're mainly books destined for shelves that don't yet exist and the dining room doesn't really matter. We don't exactly dine in style.'

'Shame on you,' Anna teased, then cocked her head on one side. 'Can I help?'

'Please—put the kettle on. I just want to put the frozen stuff away and check the kids, then we'll sit down for a bit of peace and quiet.'

She looked around at the kitchen. It was lovely, but it needed help. The units were awful, but they were easily replaced, and if the doorway from the breakfast area could be moved to the other side of the chimney breast, then the table could sit by the window and that would be much better.

The house looked, from the little she'd seen, as if it had been 'modernised' in the fifties, and it certainly needed some sympathetic restoration, but the potential was huge. Her curiosity was running riot. What was the rest of the house like?

'Right, that's that lot. How's the kettle?'

'Not boiled,' she told him. 'Can I have a guided tour?'

His face fell comically. 'Oh, lord,' he groaned, rolling his eyes in obvious embarrassment. 'I hate to think what a mess it is, and Helle's rooms will be chaos gone mad.'

'I'm not looking at the mess—I'm looking at the house, at the potential,' she coaxed, her avid curiosity unwilling to remain unsatisfied. 'If you really, really mind I'll let you say no, but I'd love to see it if you can bring yourself to let me.'

He hovered, just for a second, then squared his shoulders. 'Oh, what the heck, come on, then. Just don't say I didn't warn you,' he grumbled, and she laughed softly.

'I promise.'

'You can give me some advice. Skye's bedroom is first on the list, and I don't know what to do.'

'Ask her,' Anna said promptly, cautious of

becoming involved. 'It's her room—she's more than old enough to have ideas.'

'If only she would share them,' he murmured. 'Come on, then, let's get this over with.'

Anna went up the stairs after him and followed him straight down the landing and into Skye's bedroom. It was above the kitchen and overlooked the back garden, heavily shadowed now in the dark but fascinating to Anna for all that. She'd glimpsed it from the kitchen and itched to explore it in daylight. Her own garden was tiny, and she'd always thought she'd love a bigger garden. She tried not to envy him.

Skye was sitting on the bed, still fully dressed, colouring in a book. She glanced up and then looked away, dismissing them.

'I'm showing Anna the house,' Adam told her. 'Is it OK to come in?'

She shrugged.

'I'm sorry, it's an awful cheek—Skye, do you mind?' Anna asked, wary of stepping on clearly sensitive little toes.

She shrugged again, noncommitally, and carried on colouring. Anna looked around. It was desperately in need of love and attention, but it was bigger than Anna's sitting room, and way bigger than her bedrooms had ever been. There was a pretty little fireplace against one wall, cast iron and delicately patterned inset tiles, and Anna would have given her eye teeth for it as a child. As an adult, in fact!

'What a wonderful room—it's huge,' she said with genuine awe. 'My bedroom at home is much smaller!'

'Before, I had to share with the boys,' Skye said, clearly impressed that her room was bigger than

Anna's. 'Well, after she went. First I had the little room, but then the au pairs had it.'

Au pairs? As in, lots of them? Of course, they didn't come for long, Anna thought, and wondered if 'she' was their mother. Inevitably. And she'd gone somewhere. Where? It was suddenly a minefield, and she picked her way through it with enormous care.

'Do you know what you want to do with it now you've got such a lovely room?' Anna asked her. 'It's all yours—it must be wonderful, I should think, to be able to choose.'

Skye shrugged. 'Don't know.' She seemed to withdraw into herself then, as if too much attention was focused on her, and Anna gave a slight smile and moved further away, giving her room.

'I'm sure you'll have lots of fun deciding. I always think that's the best bit.' She turned towards Adam and pushed him gently towards the door. 'Come on, let's leave her in peace. I want to see the rest. What's next?'

He showed her the loo and bathroom, both in need of tidying up and probably refitting in a more sympathetic style than the ugly suite that was there. Still, it worked, she supposed, except for the dripping tap, although an Edwardian original would have been more attractive.

'I'm going to refit it when I get time,' he told her. 'I thought I might rearrange it to fit a loo in here as well—it seems silly not to have one in the bathroom, and there's tons of room.'

'Can you do plumbing?' she asked, impressed, and he laughed.

'Me? I'm an orthopaedic surgeon, don't forget. I'm

a dab hand with a saw and a screwdriver, and I'm good at plugging vascular leaks, too.'

'Hmm. Let's just hope your pipes heal,' she said with a smile, and he chuckled.

'They won't need to. You wait, it'll be perfect. Come and see the rest.'

He took her into the boys' room, and they were much more welcoming and extrovert than Skye had been. She was shown their toys, and how each of them had their own space in a corner of the even bigger room, and they bounced around and generally didn't look ready for bed.

'Your teacher's going to complain about you being too tired in the morning, Danny,' Adam threatened mildly, but he didn't seem to be worried. 'Come on, into your pyjamas, wash your faces and clean your teeth, boys, please,' he said with more firmness, and they grumbled off to the bathroom, leaving Adam and Anna to finish the house tour.

'I don't think we should look at Helle's rooms while she's out,' Adam said thoughtfully, pausing at the foot of the attic stairs. 'It doesn't seem right.' He hesitated just a fraction, then shot her a crooked little smile. 'That just leaves mine.'

He opened the door behind him, walked in and groaned softly. Anna went up on tiptoe and peered over his shoulder.

'So you didn't make the bed—so what?' she said, and nudged him gently through the doorway. He moved out of her way, letting her see the full extent of the room, and it took her breath away.

It was lovely. Well, no, it was a mess. The walls needed papering, the curtains were ghastly, the carpet was in shreds and the colour scheme seemed to have been put together by a committee. Mentally, she painted it a soft, pale ivory cream. White, but not white. Restful. Tranquil.

Neutral carpet—jute, perhaps? Off-white curtains, soft and diaphanous, drifting in the warm spring breeze. Pale ivory bedlinen, a duvet like a cloud of thistledown—and Adam, reaching out for her.

She realised she was staring at the bed, picturing him in it, picturing *them* in it. Together. The crumpled sheets and tumbled quilt sprang into focus, and she could see the imprint of his head on one of the pillows. Her breath jammed in her throat and she looked round a little wildly.

A door caught her eye. 'What's in there?' she asked, desperate for something else to think about—anything else except that rumpled, evocative bed!

'The shower room.'

'May I?' Anna crossed to it without waiting for his permission, opened the door and found herself in a narrow little room, functional but tired. She turned and smacked straight into his chest, her hands flying up to act as buffers.

They landed lightly on Adam's ribcage, splayed out over the broad expanse of bone and muscle that her fingers itched to explore, and with a tiny sigh she stepped back and dropped her hands. 'Sorry,' she murmured.

She glanced up at him, and her eyes locked with his. They were burning, dark and smoky, and sending a thousand conflicting messages.

'Anna?' he said softly.

She could never work out afterwards which one of them moved first, but somehow they ended up together, her hands pillowed lightly on his chest again, his hands coming up to frame her face with gentle, reverent fingers that drew her closer.

His mouth hovered for an instant, then he closed his eyes and lowered his head that last, tiny distance.

Heat. So much heat, so carefully controlled. His lips were soft, feather-light, coaxing and promising, and Anna felt need rip through her like a tidal wave. Her fingers curled, clinging to him, bunching his sweater in both hands and hanging on for dear life.

Of their own accord her lips parted, and with a soft sigh he traced the moist inner edge of her mouth with his tongue.

It wasn't enough. Holding his sweater wasn't enough. She dropped it, sliding her arms up and locking them behind his head, drawing him down closer. Her body arched against his, and with a ragged sigh he wrapped his arms around her, cupping her bottom and lifting her against the cradle of his thighs.

'Anna,' he groaned, and his mouth took hers, finally given free rein.

It was glorious. She lost touch with everything except the feel of his body hard and needy against hers, as needy as her own, aching and longing and desperate.

Then abruptly, without warning, Adam lifted his head and released her, backing away. His eyes were tortured, the hard planes of his cheeks drawn taut with emotion.

'The children,' he muttered unsteadily, and she became dimly aware of the boys screaming and Skye reasoning with them.

What had they been thinking about? 'You'd better go and sort them out,' she said in a voice that didn't quite seem to belong to her.

He rammed his hands in his pockets and stepped back further, tipping his head back and dragging in lungfuls of air. 'I'm sorry,' he grated, and, turning on his heel, he went out, leaving her alone to gather the shreds of her composure around her.

She turned slowly, looking at herself in the mirror over the basin. The light was unforgiving, showing clearly her lips, slightly bruised and swollen with passion, her eyes clouded and confused, her skin flushed where his stubble had scraped her.

She looked definitively kissed, she thought, and the tiny bubble of hysterical laughter broke as a strangled sob. She splashed cold water on her face, blotted it dry with a towel that was still damp—from his shower?

The thought did nothing for her composure.

She went back into the bedroom and looked around, and suddenly the bleak emptiness of it struck her like a blow. There was the bed, a simple, ordinary divan with a velvet headboard, a chest of drawers that had seen better days but which with attention could be lovely, a lightweight chair that had a shirt abandoned on it, one sleeve trailing on the floor. And, apart from the fitted cupboards each side of the delicate tiled fireplace, that was it.

It was a huge room, and it had a bed, a chair and a chest. No pictures, no lamps, no *pair* of chairs, no his and hers dressing-gowns dropped across the foot of the bed—just the bare essentials for a lonely man struggling to do the best for his family.

She felt tears welling up to blind her, and dragged in a deep breath to stem them before she made a fool of herself.

Just in the nick of time. Adam put his head round

the door and gave her an apologetic smile. 'You OK?' he asked in a gruff undertone.

Anna nodded. 'Yes—thanks. Do you need a hand?'

He shook his head. 'They're all done. I'm going to make some coffee, or would you rather have tea?'

She smiled. 'Tea, please. I'll come down.'

Odd, how one kiss could make so much difference. He hadn't known what to say to her, and she left just as soon as she'd drunk the tea. He didn't kiss her goodnight—well, a light brush of his lips over her forehead, all he dared to do for fear of losing control.

She'd awakened a raging demon in him that screamed for fulfilment, and he needed time to wrestle it back under control before he dared to touch her again.

He should never have asked her back for coffee. It had been a foolish thing to do, too risky in the raw emotional state he was in. Asking for trouble.

He went up to his room, uncaring that Helle was still out and would probably wake him yet again on the way in. It seemed unlikely that he would be asleep.

As he opened the door, he was hit like a sledgehammer by the image of Anna standing there, her arms wrapped tightly round her slender body, her eyes shimmering with tears. He'd wanted to kiss them away, to lay her down on the bed behind her and love her till all her tears were dry and she slept peacefully in his arms.

The longing ache nearly undid him. He sagged against the wall, his head dropped back, eyes sightless. All he could see was her mouth, soft and ripe, just before he'd kissed her. He'd felt the soft press of her breasts pillowed against him, and his hands had itched to know them, to feel the heavy fullness of them in his palms, to lower his head and take them in turn into his mouth and suckle her…

He turned and slammed his fist against the wall in empty frustration. Why here? Why in this room, where nothing would distract him from the memory of her pliant, willing body arching against him?

He groaned and threw off his clothes, showered—hot water, because he knew it would take the melt waters of the Arctic to make any difference—and crawled into his unmade bed, dragging the quilt up round his shoulders against the cold and burrowing down into the pillows, trying to escape.

He couldn't. The image was too powerful, too fresh, too necessary to his starving body for him to let it go.

So he lay there, thinking of Anna, and even the incessant clamouring of his body couldn't drown out the empty ache in his heart—an ache that he was suddenly very afraid only she would be able to fill.

He needed her. In so very many ways, he needed her, but the children came first. They had to.

For the thousandth time he wondered if he'd done the right thing by them in keeping them, but after nearly a year, how could he have let them go? Almost all of Jasper's life at the time? The baby hadn't known anyone else, and Danny had never been more than a couple of feet from him while he'd been awake. Even Skye, terribly wounded by the death of their mother and then Lyn's defection, had needed him, perhaps in her way even more than the others.

The last two years had been hard, but they'd got through them together and they were on the mend, all of them. He just had to be there for them, see them through.

So he had needs, too. Tough. He couldn't let that alter his course, let it hurt the children, not in any way. They were too precious and vulnerable and utterly dependent on him.

But the loneliness ate at him, and when Helle's noisy return woke him in the night his pillow was damp…

Anna contemplated skiving off.

She thought about it long and hard as she got ready for the day, but in the end she sighed, put on her coat and went to work, as she'd known she would.

Anyway, she wanted to see Adam—sort of. She wasn't sure. There'd been a lingering tension about him as they'd sat in the kitchen for their drinks. Significantly, he hadn't even suggested going into the sitting room, and she'd felt he'd wanted her out of the way, so the moment her tea had been downed she'd left.

He'd kissed her on the forehead, a light touch, too brief and yet with a curious lingering, as if he'd wanted more—much more.

Maybe too much more.

Whatever. Anna parked at the hospital, went in and shed her coat in her locker, pulled a clean, colourful tabard on over her uniform and pinned on her watch and badge.

'Just in case I forget who I am,' she often joked, but today she thought it was quite likely. It would serve to remind her that she was a work colleague, a single woman, not his wife, not Mrs Adam Bradbury.

'Anna Bradbury,' she found herself saying, testing

it, and could have thumped her head against the nearest wall. 'Leave it alone,' she growled at herself, and looked up to find Allie eyeing her with curiosity.

'You OK?' she asked doubtfully.

'I'm fine. How are you? How are the wedding plans?'

Allie pulled a wry face. 'Oh, advancing, I suppose. Mark wants to get married now in a register office, my mother wants to have the full works and palaver for her baby girl—you know how it is.'

'Yes—and your mother will win,' Anna said drily, trying not to think about marrying Adam and what sort of wedding she'd choose.

Two days, she told herself fiercely. That's all you've known him, two days. How can you even *think* about it?

Then she looked up and saw him striding onto the ward, and he smiled at her as if she was the best thing he'd seen all week, and she thought, *That's how I can think about it.*

'Hi,' he murmured once he was in earshot.

'Hi,' she replied. Her voice was catching and early-morning soft, and she felt like a lovesick fool. Still, it was wonderful to be this close to him again after—what, less than twelve hours?

You're losing it, she told herself silently.

Allie had vanished, leaving them alone in a void that pulsed with emotional and sexual tension. Adam's eyes searched hers, then with a sigh his lids slid shut briefly and he turned away. 'Um—about last night.'

Oh, hell. 'I know. It was a one-off, it didn't mean anything, forget it—is that what you're going to say?'

His smile was wry, his eyes softening with humour. 'Actually, no. I was going to ask why you ran away.'

Anna felt her brow pleat in a puzzled frown. 'I thought you wanted me to go?'

'No.' He shook his head. 'Well—I don't know. I don't know what I wanted.'

I do, she thought. I know exactly what you wanted, because I wanted it, too, and I just bet you didn't sleep a wink more than I did.

'I'm sorry I misunderstood. I'll make up for it when I've got a moment, but now I have to go and take report from the night sister. I'll catch up with you later.'

'OK. I'm busy, anyway. We'll grab a cup of tea later in the day, perhaps.' His smile curled round her heart, warming her, and she took it with her into the office, unaware of its tender reflection on her own face.

'Morning,' she said brightly. 'How's it been?'

The night nurse, Angela Davis, rolled her eyes. 'OK, if you like mayhem. You look happy.'

'I do?' How odd, Anna thought. I feel confused, not happy. Excited and scared and puzzled all at once. 'So, what's been happening?'

'All sorts. Karl Fisher's been in a lot of pain and he's been crying in the night. I got him written up for some stronger analgesia, but he's still suffering. All he can say is "I thought it was going to be better", which just makes you feel dreadful. Still, the hand looks good and sensory and motor response in it are fine, so it's just post-op pain and nothing more sinister, I'm sure. It might be an idea to get Robert Ryder or Adam Bradbury to look at him—I'm not sure who he belongs to now.'

'Neither am I,' Anna agreed. 'I'll ask Adam in a minute. He's about, I think. Anyone else been a problem? Any admissions?'

'Toby Cardew—asthma attack.'

'But he's only just gone home!' Anna exclaimed in horror. 'What triggered it—any idea?'

'None. They were muttering something about anxiety—seems like it's the only thing left.'

'I should think it is,' Anna agreed. 'They've checked all the obvious allergens and some of the less obvious, and eliminated just about everything else.'

'Quite. All that's left is exercise, and he was in bed, sleeping, anxiety, which seems possible, and meteorological changes, like humidity, for example, but as he was inside and had been for some time it seems unlikely. Whatever, he's back, he's stable now just about, but he was bad.'

Anna nodded. 'I'll go and see him—is Mum with him?'

'Yes, she's been here all night. Dad's at home with the others.'

'Fine. Anyone else?'

'Oh, yes. An appendix. Andrew Reed, aged eight—he's been to Theatre and was on the point of rupture when they opened him up, apparently. And Tim Scully, a nasty greenstick fracture of the radius and ulna—child fell out of the top bunk. First night in a new bed. Typical, isn't it? They said he was so excited about the bed he couldn't wait to get in it, and then, of course, he needed the loo during the night because he hadn't remembered to go in the excitement, and he fell getting onto the ladder, apparently.'

'Has he gone to Theatre?'

'No—he's all prepped and ready, and they've

called Adam Bradbury in to look at him. I think he's going to operate this morning. That's why Bradbury's on the ward, I think you'll find.'

And Anna had thought it had been because of her. How silly. She felt a huge wave of disappointment, and suppressed it. He had a job to do, and so did she. It wasn't just some surreal tearoom, or a film set. They finished going through the other patients, and she took the keys and the responsibility for the ward from Angela, and went to see if Adam was still about.

He was—talking to the parents of Tim Scully, the young lad who had fallen off his bunk bed, so while he finished she went to see Toby, their asthmatic. He was in a bed in a side room, propped up on the bed table, his arms folded and leaning forward on a pillow, still struggling for breath despite all the medication.

His nostrils were flaring with each inspiration, and his whole body seemed to be involved in each breath out, and she quietly went through some breathing exercises with him, trying to relax him and shift some of the mucus that was obviously blocking all his bronchial tubes.

He did manage to cough and shift some of the thickened mucus, and after that he seemed a little better. He sank back against the raised end of the bed, propped almost upright, and she tucked the bedclothes round him and left him to rest. His mother looked exhausted, and Anna took her hand and squeezed it.

'Cup of tea?' she offered, and Mrs Cardew nodded gratefully.

'Thanks. It's been another of those nights.'

'I'm sure. Why don't you try and have a nap if he goes off? It would do you good.'

She nodded. Anna found Pearl, their kind-hearted orderly, and asked her to make Mrs Cardew tea, then tracked Adam down just as he was leaving the ward.

'Hi. Can you have a look at Karl before you go?' she asked. 'He's been suffering in the night.'

'Sure.' He turned and retraced his footsteps and she fell in beside him. 'Any idea what's wrong?' he asked.

'Post-op pain. No neuro or vascular problems obvious, apparently, just pain.'

'Might be the cast.'

'They thought it was all right.'

He nodded, and stopped beside Karl's bed. 'Hello, young man. I gather you've been uncomfortable in the night.'

Karl nodded miserably. 'It really, really hurts,' he said unhappily. Adam examined the arm gently, turning it this way and that, feeling the fingers for warmth, testing the reflexes.

'Can you feel that?' he asked a few times, moving from place to place, and Karl nodded.

'Is the pain in the bone? Or is it the skin and muscles that hurt?'

'I don't know. It just hurts,' he said, and started to cry.

Adam laid a gentle hand on his shoulder and squeezed it comfortingly. 'OK. I'll give you something for the pain, then I want you to have an X-ray and see if we can find out a reason for it, and I think we'll have the cast off and look inside it in case it's too tight or your arm's just too bruised to sit inside it. You could have it in a sort of soft padded cradle beside you, but you'd have to lie very, very still for a day or two. We'll see. Let's try the painkillers and the picture first.'

He stood up and picked up the chart, scribbling down a prescription in the bold, jagged writing that was becoming familiar to Anna. 'Here—can you give him this, please, and set up the X-ray? I suppose I need to sign something to authorise that.'

His grin was infectious. 'Oh, yes,' Anna said with an answering smile. 'Of course. You have to sign for a cup of tea in this place.'

'Put me down for one later. I'll be ready for it. I'm going to do Tim's arm now. He's all prepped and ready, I gather?'

'So Angela said. What are you going to do?'

'Open reduction and internal fixation. There's no way you can get a satisfactory result with anything less. It's a heck of a fracture for such a little fall, but I think he caught it in the ladder, between the ladder and the bed, and he's quite a hefty lad. No matter, I can fix it.'

He found himself thinking of Anna as he straightened up the drastically bent and damaged bones and screwed plates onto them to hold them in place. She'd seemed pleased enough to see him, if the light in her eyes was anything to go by.

It was hard to pretend enthusiasm to that extent, he thought, turning the screw that brought the radius neatly into alignment. It didn't need to be drawn together because the bone was still connected, just badly bent, exactly like a young, green stick—hence the term greenstick fracture. He tackled the ulna, thinking still of Anna's eyes and the softness of her mouth when she'd smiled at him.

The rest of the surgical team were gossiping about someone he didn't know, and he ignored them, working steadily, thinking about the children and Helle and how he was going to get a replacement for her.

Not only how he would get a replacement, but how he would *keep* the replacement. Au pairs seemed to have a very short shelf life, and the departure of each one brought trauma and loss to the children's lives.

It was unsatisfactory for them from an emotional point of view, but he supposed it at least kept the attachments they formed fixed firmly on him, and not on the carers. That was good, because he, God willing, was going nowhere.

He straightened up, turned the limb back and forth to examine the position, checked the warmth and colour of the fingers and closed the incision, satisfied that he'd reduced the fracture to the best of his ability and that it would heal fast and well.

That was all he could do. He pulled off his mask, smiled at the team and thanked them, snapped off his gloves and dropped them in the bin with his hat and gown.

Tea with Anna, he thought, and headed back to the ward.

# CHAPTER FOUR

IT WAS the weekend. Apart from a brief cup of tea when he'd come back to the ward to talk to Tim's parents about his operation, Anna hadn't seen Adam all day. He'd been in Outpatients doing a clinic, and he hadn't reappeared.

Karl's X-rays had been sent down to him in Outpatients, and he'd sent back instructions for the cast to be removed and for the boy's arm to be rested in a padded gutter support until the following day, when it would be put in an open cast if the pain improved and the swelling of the soft tissues subsided. Apparently, when he'd been coming round from the anaesthetic he'd flung his arm against the cot-sides of the stretcher. It was possible that the cast had become slightly bent then, before it had quite hardened, and that even such very slight pressure had been enough to make Karl miserable.

Once it was removed he seemed much more comfortable, and fell asleep immediately, a sure sign that he'd had a difficult night. Tim was still largely out of it after his operation, and Andrew Reed, who'd been admitted in the night with acute appendicitis, was improving hourly.

And now it was the weekend, and she was off, by a miracle, and it stretched ahead of her emptily. The chances of bumping into Adam at the supermarket again were so slight as to be not worth considering, and, short of going round there and ringing his doorbell, she couldn't think of any way she could see him until Monday.

What on earth was she supposed to do to fill the time? She couldn't bring herself to do any of the things she normally did. They seemed so empty somehow, so fruitless.

She wondered what Adam would be doing, and if the children were looking forward to having him to themselves. Danny would be, she thought with certainty, and probably little Jaz, but Skye—Skye was a strange one, a poor, lonely little girl, very self-contained and withdrawn.

Worryingly so. In many ways, Anna thought, she probably needed her father more than the others.

Curiosity teased her again. She found herself wondering about their mother—his wife, in fact. When had she left, and why? Had she gone willingly, or had their divorce been acrimonious and bitter?

Did he still love her? That thought was oddly painful to contemplate.

She found herself remembering the kiss, going over those few brief moments in her mind for the hundredth time. Would it happen again? Oh, lord, she hoped so.

The television failed to hold her attention, and finally, at only a quarter to ten, she gave up on the evening, had a quick shower and went to bed. She had hardly put her head on the pillow when the phone rang beside her, and she propped herself up on her elbow and picked up the receiver, a little glimmer of hope edging into her heart. He didn't have her number, but…

'Hello?'

'Anna? It's Adam.'

He stopped, and she had the oddest feeling that he didn't quite know what to say. Funny, she felt the same. She said hello again, hoping she didn't sound inane and wondering if the smile on her face was obvious in her voice, and afraid that it probably was. 'How are you?' she asked, her finger winding absently into the curling flex.

'I'm fine. Look, Anna, I'm sorry to ring you at home so late—I had to do some sleuthing to get your number. I hope you don't mind.'

'Of course I don't mind.' She sat up straighter, concerned by the note in his voice, and pulled her finger free. 'Adam, is something wrong?'

He sighed, and she could visualise him stabbing his hands distractedly through that dark, silky hair. 'No, not...wrong, exactly. It's just...Helle's gone to London for the weekend, I'm supposed to be on call and the kids are with my parents just up the road. I just...'

He sighed again, and then went on, his voice soft and gruff and intimate, 'I just wanted to talk to you. The house seemed awfully empty and, well, I thought it might be nice to see you, but it's too late, really, so I thought I'd phone. Have a chat.'

He ran out of words again, and Anna pushed the quilt off her legs and swung them over the side of the bed, sitting up. 'It's not too late,' she said gently. 'Either to phone or to come round, if you want to.'

'It's after ten.'

'That doesn't matter. Do you want to come here, or do you want me to come to you?'

'I'll come to you—it seems only fair as it's my idea. It's freezing outside. I can bring my bleeper. Where are you? How do I find you?'

She gave him concise directions, ran a mental eye over the house and groaned inwardly. She could usefully have spent the last three hours doing housework instead of moping about him.

Oh, damn. There was no time to choose clothes. She pulled on her jeans and a clean jumper, pulled them off again, puffed a little cloud of perfume in the air and walked through it, then dragged the clothes back on and ran downstairs, banging cushions and tidying the kitchen rapidly.

It would take him ten minutes, tops, and she'd already been more than five.

She turned off the centre light, put on the lamps each end of the sofa, lit the fat church candles on the dresser and went to put the kettle on. She only had tea or coffee to offer him, no wine or spirits or anything like that, not even beer, but he was driving so perhaps it was just as well.

The doorbell rang, cutting off her stream of panic, and she paused for a second, drew a steadying breath, ran her hands down her jeans in case the palms were clammy and went to the door, swinging it open with a welcoming smile.

He looked wonderful. He was untidy, his hair rumpled, the poloneck of his sweater rolled over crookedly, but his eyes would have put the Olympic torch to shame and his mouth...

She drew him in, went up on tiptoe and kissed it, just lightly, just once, but it was enough. He dropped something that landed with a soft thud, and then she was in his arms and his mouth was on hers and she could stop fantasising about his kiss because it was happening again and it was real, more real than she thought she could bear.

Then he lifted his head, gave her a crooked smile and bent and picked up the thing he'd dropped. 'Here, for you. Sorry, the corner's bent but I don't suppose it matters. I got, um, distracted.'

Chocolates. Sinful, decadent chocolates, not just ordinary ones but deep, dark continental liqueur chocolates with a zillion calories each. 'How on earth did you know?' she said with a laugh, and looked up into his wonderfully expressive eyes and forgot to breathe again for a moment.

'I didn't—I just guessed,' Adam confessed gruffly. 'I would have brought wine, but I'm driving and I thought the chocolates would be a nice compromise.'

'Thank you.' Anna went up on tiptoe and kissed him again, then took his arm and drew him into her living room. 'Sit down, I'll get you a drink. Tea or coffee? It's all I've got, I'm afraid, unless you want water or fruit juice?'

'Coffee'll be fine. Let me help you make it.'

'Oh, the kitchen's a mess—'

He laughed softly, cutting her off. 'Fair's fair. You saw my house at its absolute worst yesterday.'

'But I've got no excuse,' she protested.

Hmm. He was just as stubborn as her, obviously, because he turned her round, put his hands on her shoulders and propelled her gently back out into the hall and down to the kitchen.

'It looks fine—what are you talking about?' he said from right behind her, his breath puffing softly against her nape. She had a crazy urge to lean back, just a tiny little bit, and bend her head, and let his lips stroke a trail of fire over her skin…

As if she'd willed it, she felt his lips against her hair, his touch like the brush of an angel's wing, so light yet with so much power. Her eyes drifted shut and she stood motionless as his hands eased her back against him, so she could feel the heat of his body through her thin sweater, warming her.

His lips moved lower, caressing the sensitive skin of her nape, hot and slow and unbelievably erotic. His tongue traced a pattern on the skin, then he blew, just softly, and she felt the touch of ice over the fire.

'You're beautiful,' he murmured, and his voice was husky with promise.

Her breath jammed in her throat. Make love to me, she thought. Don't stop. Take me to heaven. Please…

He let her go, stepping just out of reach and leaving her abandoned in a sea of emotion so powerful she thought she'd drown. 'Coffee?' he said softly, and she moved then, like an automaton, taking mugs from the cupboard, finding the coffee, a spoon, sugar.

'Do you want sugar in your coffee?' she asked, realising she'd never made it for him. She'd hardly done anything for him. She'd known him three days!

Just three short days, and yet she knew he was more important to her than anyone else she'd ever met. OK, it was hasty, it was foolish and impulsive and precipitate and all the other things that her mother would have warned her about, but it was also *right*.

She turned to give him his coffee, and found him watching her with a strangely intense expression. He took the mug from her and put it down.

'No, I don't want sugar. I want to make love to you, but it's too soon,' he said gruffly. His honesty rocked her, and brought tears to her eyes.

'No, it's not,' she said, with a matching honesty. 'It's not too soon—not for us. I feel as if I've been waiting for you for years.'

For a moment Adam said nothing, then the breath left him in a rush and he closed his eyes. When he opened them again the heat in them consumed Anna. He held out his hand, and wordlessly she went to him, placing her hand in his and leading him upstairs to her bedroom.

In the doorway, she hesitated. 'It's a mess,' she said softly, and he gave a strangled laugh.

'Do you really think I care?' He turned her, his eyes searching hers, and she knew he could see only her. 'Oh, Anna,' he whispered, and drew her into his arms. His mouth found hers, and his kiss was tender. 'I didn't come here for this,' he murmured gruffly. 'That's not why I rang you—'

'Shh. It's all right, I know.' She lifted her hand, her fingertips searching his face, stroking the line of his cheekbone, the muscle jumping in his jaw, rubbing lightly backwards against the rasp of stubble, somehow so erotic against her skin. Her hand slid round to cradle his nape and draw him down to her again. 'Make love to me,' she murmured. 'Please. Now. I need you.'

His eyes flared and darkened, and with a ragged groan he sought her mouth and took it. Fire seemed to rip through her, and her legs buckled and gave way.

He caught her against him, lifting her and setting her down gently in the middle of her tumbled bed. He undressed her slowly, his fingers shaking, and she could see from the harsh rise and fall of his chest how aroused he was, just how much effort it took to hold on to his control.

'You are so lovely,' he whispered unsteadily. His eyes tracked over her, then locked with hers, and the raw hunger in them found an echo in her heart. 'Anna, I need you.'

'I know. It's OK.' She knelt up in the middle of the bed and seized the hem of his sweater, dragging it over his head with a total lack of ceremony. Her patience, such as it was, was at an end, and she needed him now, needed to hold him, to touch him, to be part of him. Nothing else mattered, and no other thought entered her head.

She stripped him, her breath jamming in her chest at the sight of his body, lean and muscled and so, so ready. She touched him with trembling hands, feeling the hot satin of his skin under her palms, the shudder as she skimmed her fingers over him, learning him, treasuring him with her touch.

'Anna,' he whispered, his breath jagged, his control in tatters. Good. That was what she wanted. She didn't want technique, she didn't want skill, she wanted him. Just him. Nothing more, nothing less.

'Yes,' she answered, and drew him down into her arms...

Boneless.

She was curled into his side, her head cradled on his chest and one knee wedged between his thighs. They were just about as close as they could get, and about as drained. Gradually Anna's senses returned, her breathing slowed, her heart settled to a steady rhythm. Adam's was beating just under her ear, slow and strangely comforting.

She didn't move. She couldn't move. She just lay there, like an abandoned doll, sprawled against him and listening to his heartbeat. She felt his hand on her back, gliding slowly over the skin, caressing her absently. She gave a soft sigh of contentment, and he turned his head, pressing his lips to her forehead.

'OK?'

'How can you even ask that?' she mumbled, too slaked to move her mouth properly.

A low chuckle rumbled through his chest, and he hugged her closer, pulling the covers over her and tucking them round her shoulders. 'It was pretty spectacular, wasn't it?'

Something niggled at her—something important—but she couldn't think what it was or deal with it. She closed her eyes, squirmed a little closer to him and sighed again. Biology was a very clever thing, she thought idly, and then remembered what it was that was niggling her.

Oh, damn.

Her finger outlined a pattern on his chest. 'Um...did I miss something, or did we just forget to use anything?' she asked quietly.

He went still, his hand on her back coming to rest where it was, his breathing suspended for a second. Then he moved again, his hand resuming its gentle rhythm against her spine. 'No, you didn't miss anything, Anna, but it's OK. You aren't going to catch anything from me.'

'Catch anything?' she repeated, puzzled. She wasn't thinking about catching so much as falling.

'The last woman I slept with was my wife, over three years ago,' he confessed. 'You're safe.'

Three years? No wonder he'd been so responsive to her touch! And her to his, of course. Between them they'd stacked up a lot of years of abstinence. Small surprise that their lovemaking had packed such a punch.

'I was more worried about getting pregnant,' she explained. 'I'm not on the Pill.'

Again Adam went still, and then he spoke, his voice flat and expressionless. 'There's no need. When I said you're safe, I meant it in every sense. I can't get you pregnant, Anna. I'm sterile.'

Shock held her motionless for several seconds, then her breath left her as if her lungs had been punctured.

Sterile?

Adam, sterile? Adam, who had three children, couldn't get her pregnant?

'But you've got three children,' Anna said in confusion. 'How come…?'

'They're adopted.'

'Oh.' What else was there to say? She dragged in a deep breath, and let it out in a shaky gust. 'Are you sure?'

'That they're adopted? Absolutely,' he said, a thread of humourless laughter in his voice.

'No—I meant—that you can't have children,' she said, hardly able to say the words. There was a huge, empty void opening up inside her, and she was desperate to stop it spreading because she knew it would consume her. She wanted his child—*needed* his child.

'Yes, I'm sure,' he said quietly after a moment, and she could hear the pain in his voice. She put her own pain on one side and concentrated on his. She could deal with hers later. This was important.

'What happened?' she asked gently. 'Do you know?'

'I had mumps when I was twenty-five. I was really ill with it—I'd never had it and we visited my wife's sister. Her children went down with it just after we'd left them and, of course, I'd picked it up. I developed severe orchitis as a complication, and then a few months afterwards when we decided to start a family, nothing happened.'

'So you had a test.'

'Yes. They found very few healthy sperm. Low motility, that sort of thing. Lyn was gutted. We tried everything—crazy positions, centrifugal spinning to concentrate the sperm, syringes—all sorts. We didn't make love for years. We had sex—carefully orchestrated sex timed to coincide with her ovulation, not a single sperm wasted on frivolous entertainment, and month after month we failed. We couldn't go down the IVF or ICSI route, because the treatment didn't agree with her, so that was that.'

Anna swallowed the tears that were hovering in her throat and threatening to choke her. 'So you decided to adopt.'

'Yes. We decided to adopt. We went through all the screening procedures with all their intrusive and highly personal investigations, and shortly before we were approved we were given some catalogues of children—the kids nobody wanted. They're called "Children Who Wait", and there is simply page after page of tragedy. They're mostly families, because they're the hardest to home. Nobody wants a family group. They want a baby. We were looking for a baby, just one, and then we saw my three and I just fell for them. I knew they were right.'

'What did Lyn think?'

He shrugged. 'I don't know. At the time she agreed to try, but she never seemed too wholehearted—it was always me. I should have listened to her, I suppose. She had reservations for good reasons. I had none. I knew we could give those children a good home.'

'How old were they?' Anna asked, trying to picture the sorry little family.

'Skye was three, Danny not quite two and Jaz was a little baby. Their mother was dead, a drugs overdose, and there was no father figure in evidence. It was a cut-and-dried adoption with no strings—it should have been easy. Instead, it drove us apart, although I didn't realise it at the time. I was too taken up with the children to see the signs, and we were in the process of finalising the adoption when Lyn left me.'

Even now, after all this time, Anna could hear the hurt in his voice. There was more to the story, she could tell, but not even she could have guessed the full extent of the hurt Lyn had inflicted on them.

'Was it very bitter?' she asked gently.

'Bitter?' Adam dragged in a deep breath and let it go on a harsh gust of laughter. 'You could say that. She went off with my best friend,' he said rawly. 'They'd been having an affair for months. She was pregnant.'

Her eyes closed to keep out the horror of his words, but they swirled round in her head, shocking in their simplicity. 'Oh, Adam,' she said brokenly, and slid her arms round him to hold him close. 'I'm so, so sorry.'

His grip tightened. 'It's OK. I got over it. I continued with the adoption, with the reluctant blessing of Social Services, and we struggled through and we're coming out of it now. Danny was all right, more or less, but Jasper was lost without Lyn and Skye was devastated.'

'I can imagine that,' Anna said sadly. 'Poor little girl.'

'She was. She'd just started to come out of herself and thaw with us, and she was right back to square one. Worse, really, because her mother had died and been taken from her. Lyn had *chosen* to leave. That was harder to take. Skye was very, very hurt, and very difficult, and she still is.'

'And you? Were you very hurt?'

He nodded slowly. 'At the time. Betrayed more than anything else. I could understand about the baby. I knew how important it was to her—she used to say she had a biological ache to carry a child. I understood that. I had a biological ache to be a father, to see my wife swell with my child, to hold my baby in my arms. I love children. I really, really wanted a child of my own, but it couldn't happen for me.'

He broke off and took a steadying breath. 'I'm sorry, it still gets to me,' he said roughly.

'That's OK,' she murmured soothingly, her soft heart aching for him. 'Take your time, I'm not going anywhere.'

She thought he'd ground to a halt, but then after a moment Adam continued his heartbreaking story.

'I offered to let her go. When we found out it was me, I offered to divorce her if that was what she wanted. She said it wasn't. We went through the infertility programme, and again I asked her, before we started the adoption proceedings. She said no. She said no, and yet, once the children were there, living with us, and they'd been with us nearly a year—then, of all times, she turned round and said she wanted to go and that she was carrying someone else's child.

'I can't forgive her for that—for what she did to those poor, vulnerable little children—and I can't forgive my closest, oldest friend for being a part of it—

for lying to me, for listening to me unburden myself and pretending to sympathise, and then, when my back was turned, for sleeping with my wife. I nearly killed the bastard for that.'

Anna said nothing. There was nothing to say, nothing she could add that wouldn't sound trite or insincere.

'I'm sorry,' he went on after a moment. 'I don't talk about it very often, and it still gets to me.'

'Do you ever see them?'

'No. I can't forgive them for what they did to the children, and it would be hypocritical to have anything to do with them. Anyway, I'm not a sucker for punishment.' He turned his head and kissed her gently. 'I'm sorry, Anna. This all got rather heavy. I didn't mean to unload on you like that, but you may as well know the whole story.'

'Don't apologise,' she murmured. 'I've been wondering why she left. Now I know.' Knew more than she'd ever wanted to know.

Adam shifted slightly, turning towards her, and trailed a feathery kiss across her brow. 'Anyway, it's nothing to do with us,' he said softly. 'It's all gone. Finished.' He kissed her again, over her eyes, down the line of her jaw, in the soft hollow of her throat. 'Forget about it now. Let me make love to you again.'

Forget about it. Just like that, as if it was so easy.

But he was right. She would forget it now, and concentrate on him, and this moment, and then later, when she was alone, she'd deal with it.

His mouth was tracing a line of fire over her shoulder and down her arm, then back again to claim her lips. The fire spread through her body, and she arched against him, suddenly desperate to hold him close.

And then in the distance they heard his bleeper, and with a muttered curse he rolled away from her and grabbed his underwear.

'Don't move,' he instructed, and ran downstairs. She heard his voice on the phone, and then a moment later his footsteps on the stairs.

'I have to go in,' he said gruffly. 'Stay there. I'll ring you if it's going to be brief. Otherwise I'll see you tomorrow. OK?'

She nodded. 'OK.' She nearly told him to come back anyway, at whatever time, but then she thought better of it. She needed to be alone. She had a lot of thinking to do.

He tugged his sweater over his head, turned the roll-neck down and bent to kiss her goodbye.

'I'll see you later. Think of me.'

As if she could do anything else, with her body still humming from his loving and her heart in shock.

She waited till the door closed behind him, then got up and put on her dressing-gown and went downstairs. The candles were still burning, mellow pools of golden light flickering against the wall. She turned off the side lamps and curled up, opening the chocolates. They'd been going to share them over coffee, but the coffee was sitting, cold, on the side in the kitchen and he was gone.

Adam's words stayed with her, though, echoing in her head like a death knell. 'I'm sterile. I can't get you pregnant. *I'm sterile—sterile—sterile…*'

Anna swallowed, but the tears fell anyway, dripping off her chin and splashing heavily on her hands. She was grieving, she realised dimly—grieving for Adam and for the children he would never have, and for Lyn, denied her husband's child, and for herself, for the fledgling dreams that had been trampled in the dust.

The phone rang, and she answered it, gulping down the tears.

It was Adam. 'It's going to be a long night,' he said apologetically. 'Don't wait up. I'll ring you tomorrow. Save me some of the chocolates.'

'OK,' she promised, trying to inject a cheerful note into her voice. 'See you tomorrow.'

She hung up just before the sob broke, and, curling up in the corner of the settee, she finally gave in to the tears.

# CHAPTER FIVE

IT WAS a long and tragic night. Adam struggled to save the legs of a young woman involved in a car accident, while another team lost the battle for her fiancé's life in the next theatre.

He had to amputate one leg in the end, because he was unable to restore the circulation, and the other would be permanently disfigured and might well prove too difficult to treat successfully.

He did his best—he always did his best, but sometimes it just wasn't good enough, and it grieved him. She was twenty-two, a lovely girl poised on the brink of the rest of her life, and suddenly that life had been trashed by an act of fate.

And he wasn't even supposed to be operating on her! He'd come in to see a child with a pelvic fracture which hadn't need surgery in the end, and he'd been asked to stay to help because the orthopaedic team were at full stretch with a succession of RTAs.

So there he was, with a beautiful young woman needing his help and no way of undoing the damage that had been done, and he thought of Anna at home and her beautiful legs and how devastating it would be for her, and he felt gutted.

It was five o'clock in the morning before he finished, and he talked to the woman's devastated parents until nearly six. Then he showered and dressed before leaving the hospital, his thoughts still with Anna.

It was hideously early—too early to go round there—but he found himself headed in that direction anyway. He just needed to see Anna, to hold her, to be with her. It had been such a bloody night, and he needed her warmth and gentleness.

He rang the doorbell, and after a moment she appeared, looking sleepy and rumpled and pleased to see him.

'I'm sorry. I know I said I'd ring, but I just wanted to see you.'

She looked at him searchingly, understanding in her eyes. 'Bad night?'

He nodded. He didn't want to go into details. He wanted to leave it behind, to take her in his arms and finish what he'd started.

'Any chocolates left?'

She smiled guiltily. 'A few. They're in here—I fell asleep on the settee.'

He followed her into the sitting room, lit only by the two candles which had burned almost down to the end. One was spluttering, the other not far behind.

'Coffee?' she offered, and he smiled wearily.

'I've got a distinct feeling of *déjà vu*,' he said with a chuckle. 'Perhaps I'd better have tea. Might be safer.'

'Stay here. Eat the chocolates.'

'I will.' He sank wearily into a chair and helped himself. Cognac and chocolate on an empty stomach and no sleep was a lousy combination. He tried the Grand Marnier instead, and then Drambuie. No better. What he needed was sleep.

Anna came back, a tray in her hands with two gently steaming mugs, a milk jug and a pot of tea.

'For refills,' she explained, and he gave a tired smile.

'Why don't we take it upstairs to bed with the chocolates?' he suggested.

It was a good idea—at least, in theory. In practice it was too comfortable. He drank the first mug of tea, ate one more chocolate and then fell asleep with Anna snuggled up against his chest, waiting for the next mug of tea to cool.

By the time they woke it was stone cold, the sun was streaming in through a crack in the curtains and he was due at his parents' for lunch in less than an hour. He stared at his watch in disbelief, dropped his head back on the pillows and sighed.

'What's wrong?' Anna asked sleepily, raising her head from his chest to look down into his eyes.

'Nothing,' Adam said. He lifted a hand to brush her hair back off her face so he could see her better. She looked wonderful—soft and warm and creased with sleep. 'Nothing,' he repeated more softly, and felt a great wave of tenderness sweep over him. 'I have to go soon, but not yet. Not before I make love to you.'

He lifted himself up on one elbow, rolling her onto her back so he could touch her and see her. Her dressing gown was gaping slightly, and he eased the sides apart, his breath catching at the sight of her pale, slender body. He blew a thin stream of air over her nipples and they peaked for him, bringing a smile to his face.

'You're lovely,' he said softly, and, bending his head, he kissed her.

Anna felt as if she was on an emotional roller-coaster. On the one hand, she'd had the best and most wonderful weekend of her life. On the other hand, underlying it was a deep sadness, a coming to terms with all that could never be.

How bittersweet, she thought, that when she finally met the man of her dreams, he had one fatal flaw—he couldn't make the rest of her dreams come true. Of course, he had children, three lovely children who had already captured her heart, but it wasn't the same as having a baby of her own.

If she stayed with Adam, if their love grew, she would never have a child of her own, would never know the joy of carrying a growing baby inside her, of suckling it at her breast, or witnessing the first tooth, the first step, the first word. It had been her expectation, as it was every woman's expectation, that one day she'd marry and have children. Yet, if she married Adam—and it was far too soon to be thinking about that yet—that expectation would never come to fruition.

And yet, even after just one weekend, the prospect of not being with him was unthinkable. But would their love grow? Was it just lust, a mutual physical craving, an itch that needed scratching, or was it something deeper, more lasting, something that could stand the test of time?

Be patient, she told herself. Give it time to reveal itself.

But patience wasn't her strong point, and coupled with a lack of sleep it did nothing for her temper.

'I thought you'd just had a weekend off?' Allie said cheerfully, looking disgustingly happy for that time of the morning.

'I have,' Anna told her with a wry smile. 'I'm sorry. Am I being a grump?'

'Only slightly drastically. Anything to do with our gorgeous new consultant?' she added in a soft sing-song voice that had colour rushing to Anna's cheeks. Allie's eyes widened.

'Good grief!' she exclaimed in a stage whisper. 'What on earth were you two up to? I've never, *ever* seen you blush!'

'Allie, shut up,' Anna growled suppressively. 'I don't want the world to know.'

Allie cocked her head on one side and grinned. 'So there is something to know, then?'

What was it in her face that gave her away? Whatever it was, Allie's eyes softened and she pulled an apologetic face. 'I'm sorry. I'm being nosy—not that you did any such thing when I first started going out with Mark...'

'That was fair game—you'd known him for five years! I've only just met Adam.'

'No,' Allie corrected her, 'I'd known him briefly *five years ago*. That's different—and, anyway, so what? When it's right, it's right. I knew when I was eighteen that Mark was right for me.'

Anna put down the notes she was checking and gave Allie a wry smile. 'Funny, isn't it? I took one look at him, and I thought Adam was right for me. Now I'm even more sure, but—' She broke off, unable to tell Allie the personal things Adam had revealed to her.

'But?'

She shrugged. 'Allie, I can't—'

'Is it his kids? Is the ex-wife a pain?'

'It's complicated,' Anna said evasively. 'I can't explain. He told me things that I can't discuss with you, Allie.'

'He's not still married?' Allie asked, horrified, and Anna shook her head.

'No. Nothing like that. Forget it. It doesn't matter.'

And it didn't, she told herself again a few minutes later when Adam came on to the ward. It didn't matter at all, not compared to the joy of being with him and the love they could share.

What an astonishing discovery...

It was a difficult day. Adam was in and out of the ward—mostly out, because he was operating that morning—but when he was there and he saw Anna, it was as if the sun had come out.

He told Karl Fisher he could go home with a new cast on now that his pain had subsided, and little David Chisholm with his club foot operation had been discharged over the weekend. Tim Scully's greenstick fracture was settling down, and he, too, was going home with a closed cast—and with strict instructions to sleep in the bottom bunk until he was more mobile!

Anna offered Adam a cup of tea before he went up to Theatre, but he didn't have time. Today's list was short but complicated, and he wanted to get on with it. His patients were prepped, he'd seen their parents and gone over the cases again, and now he wanted to get started.

His first case was a fourteen-year-old girl with one leg seven centimetres shorter than the other. It had been fractured across the lower growth plate of her femur when she was eight and had stopped growing, and now she was having an operation to elongate it. This involved cutting through the thigh bone, putting an external support on the bone and turning a key every day just a fraction. As the bone tried to heal, so the gap would increase again and the bone would have to grow a little more to fill it.

And thus, if all went well, the leg would become at least nearly as long as the other one, if not the same length.

Bones, though, were easy. It was the muscles and nerves that caused more of a problem, and sometimes the pain of stretching them proved too much and treatment had to stop. Because of this, his patient had been doing lots of stretching exercises to her short leg to encourage the tissues to give in advance so that it was less of a shock to them. Hopefully, it would provide enough leeway to make a useful improvement.

Adam saw her in the anteroom, just before her anaesthetic, and smiled at her encouragingly. 'Hello again, Kate. All right?'

She nodded a little nervously. 'Bit scared.'

'I'm sure. Don't worry, I'll look after you. It'll be a bit rough for a day or two, but I'm sure it will be worth it.'

He winked at her mother, who was hovering distractedly by her side and trying to be brave, and she smiled back. She was near to tears, poor woman. 'Don't worry,' he told her as Kate slipped quietly into anaesthesia. 'She'll be all right. I'll come and see you as soon as we've finished.'

It was straightforward, to his relief. He exposed the bone, making a staggered cut through it so that as it extended, the ends would still overlap, giving greater support than a straight cut through the shaft would have done. He closed the wound, attached the external fixator with the help of the X-ray machine to make sure that the alignment of the bone was good, and got her out of Theatre in a shorter time than he'd anticipated.

That was good, because the next case would be long and difficult and he was impatient to start it.

A young lad with scoliosis had been referred to him for correction of the lateral curvature of his spine. It was quite severe, and with earlier intervention could have been helped considerably, but his ribs were twisting and consequently his chest was being compromised.

And now he had to be straightened, in a two-part operation over the next few weeks. Today was the first part, and he would have a rod wired to his spine all through the length of the twisted part, and by tightening up the wires the bones could be slowly persuaded into line.

He would need fixed halo-pelvic traction afterwards to help keep the spine straight, and gradually the curve would surrender and could be straightened further in a subsequent operation.

It was tricky, and it could result in paralysis if it went wrong. Nevertheless, such complex spinal surgery was his speciality and what Adam loved to do, because it made such a difference to the mental and physical well-being of the children he treated. Success wasn't guaranteed, though, and that kept a nice professional edge on the proceedings and added challenge.

Adam liked a challenge, and as he opened young Damian George's spine his focus became absolute. He forgot Anna, he forgot the children—he forgot everything except the bones and muscles under his hands, and the child in his care.

* * *

Damian had been gone for hours, Anna realised. It was three o'clock, and she was due to go off duty, but she hung on, wondering how Damian was doing and cherishing a foolish hope that Adam would come onto the ward to see him.

She was in the kitchen, making a cup of tea, when he appeared behind her, coming up close and cupping his hands over her shoulders. His fingers squeezed gently in greeting.

'Hi,' he murmured softly.

She gave in to the urge to sink back against him for a moment, and dropped her head back against his chest. 'Hi. How did it go?'

'Long and slow,' he said wearily. 'It was worse than it looked on the X-rays. I had to trim and prune quite a lot to get the result I wanted—hopefully, it'll pull straighter now. His ribs were pretty messy. Still, they should work better now, they're actually free to float, or they will be.'

'Is he here?'

'No, he's still in Recovery. He took quite a hammering under the anaesthetic. I just came to see my favourite nurse. Is that tea for me?'

She smiled and turned so she was facing him, with hardly the thickness of a piece of paper between them. 'It can be. What's it worth?'

He chuckled, his eyes glittering with intent, just as the door opened.

'That's enough of that—break it up. What's going on in here?'

Anna chuckled and slid sideways out of Adam's reach. 'Wouldn't you like to know? Hello, Josh. Good holiday?'

'Wonderful.' He buzzed her cheek with a kiss and gave Adam a thoughtful look. 'Missed me?'

'Not so as you'd notice. It's actually been quite peaceful. I don't believe you two have met—Josh, this is Adam Bradbury, the new orthopaedic consultant in paeds. Adam, meet Josh Lancaster, one of our consultant paediatricians. I thought you were due back for this morning?' she added curiously to Josh.

'We were. Plane was delayed—we landed at Heathrow at six this morning, and I came straight here. I've been in a clinic, trying to catch up, and Lissa's taken the children home to put them to bed. No doubt they'll be up all night.'

'No doubt,' Anna said with a laugh. 'Got time for tea?'

'I'll make time. So, Adam, what do you think of the Audley Memorial?'

'Well, the nursing staff are very obliging,' he said with a slow, lazy smile, and Anna turned quickly away before Josh could catch the laughing look in her eye.

She was too slow. His curiosity aroused, he hung around, so there was no opportunity for an intimate chat with Adam. They talked about the hospital, and where Adam had been before, and then Adam put his mug in the sink, kissed her on the cheek and said softly, 'I have to go and see Damian. I'll ring you tonight.'

That's blown it, she thought, and she wasn't wrong. Josh gave her a long, thoughtful look and arched a brow enquiringly.

'What?' she said crisply.

He threw up his hands. 'Nothing.'

'It's not nothing. I know you, Josh. If you've got

a problem, spit it out.' She turned to wash up Adam's mug, her back to him.

He was harder to deter than that. He picked up a teatowel and the mug, and moved to stand beside her, his back to the worktop, just in her line of sight. Patiently he wiped the mug, and Anna gave in first.

'Well?'

He lifted his shoulders. 'All a bit quick, isn't it?' he murmured. 'He only arrived on Wednesday. Here we are, the following Monday, and he's kissing you goodbye on the ward. It just seems a bit—I don't know—hasty.'

She dropped the cloth into the sink and turned slowly to face him, furious.

'Do you have a problem with that?' she asked tightly.

He shrugged again. 'A bit too much, too soon, perhaps?' he offered, and she slammed her mug into the sink, sloshing water over the edge onto the floor.

'How dare you?' she said icily. 'Who the hell appointed you my big brother anyway? And besides, you can talk! What about you and Lissa? The second night, wasn't it?'

He coloured and looked away. 'OK. Point made.'

'Bloody good job, too. Don't interfere, Josh. It's none of your damn business.'

He sighed. 'I'm sorry. I was just worrying about you, Anna. You've been getting broody. I've watched you with the kids, and you're—I don't know. You're desperate for a relationship, and I'd hate to see you rush into an affair with someone just to get pregnant.'

'Is that right?' she asked, snatching the teatowel from him and wiping out her mug with a vicious twist. 'Well, let me tell you something, buster,' she went on, pain welling up inside her. 'There's no way it's going to happen, because he can't get me pregnant, so you can save your breath!'

And spinning round, she put the mug and towel down on the worktop, put her face in her hands and howled.

'Oh, Anna.' His voice was soft, contrite, and he turned her against his chest and rocked her gently while she cried. 'Anna, I'm sorry,' he murmured. 'I had no idea.'

'Of course you had no idea!' she said crossly, pushing away from him and fumbling for a tissue in her pocket.

'Here.'

He handed her a piece of kitchen roll, and she blew her nose and wiped her eyes and glared at him again. 'Look at me, I'm a mess. I've got a kid coming back from Recovery I want to settle before I go off duty, and I look as if I've been through the wringer.'

'You needed that,' he told her gently. 'When did you find out?'

'Friday night.' She sniffed loudly and glared at him. 'And I didn't need it! For your information I've been doing it all weekend, every time Adam was out of sight! I thought I'd got over it, put it in perspective.'

He shook his head slowly. 'Anna, I'm so sorry. I suppose it's too late to tell you to leave well alone?'

She scrubbed her nose on her tissue again and pulled a face. 'What do you think?'

'I think you've given him your heart, you poor, silly girl, and I just hope he knows what a treasure he's holding in his hands.'

Damn him. It set her off again, and she got through

another two sheets of kitchen roll before she managed to pull herself together. 'How do I look?' she asked him, and he gave a wry, apologetic smile.

'Like hell.'

'Thought so.' She splashed cold water on her face, rummaged in her pocket for her rescue kit, put on a streak of lipstick and dabbed some concealer on her lower lids. 'Better?' she asked, shoving them back in her pocket.

'You've done that before?'

She smiled ruefully. 'Only every time I lose a child. Right, I have to go and settle Damian.' She went to the door, then paused, her hand on the knob. 'Josh, what I said about Adam...'

'It won't go anywhere. You know that.'

She smiled again. 'Thanks. You're a love. I'm sorry I bit your head off.'

'My pleasure,' he said with a wry chuckle. 'Any time.'

She went out into the ward and found Adam with Damian and his parents in the side ward near the nursing station. The boy was in the Stryker frame that was used for spinal cases, so that he could be turned regularly without damaging him.

He had an aluminium halo attached to his skull, and it was fixed to rods leading to another set of screws in his pelvis, holding his spine in traction. It looked far worse than it felt, but because of the pain of the spinal surgery he was attached to a syringe driver delivering painkillers in a steady, measured dose.

It would be a long, slow process to correct the spinal deformity and allow the newly remodelled bones to heal, and in the meantime he was going to be bad-tempered and tearful.

Anna had seen it all before, and knew it would present quite a nursing challenge. He was in a side room now for peace and quiet, with a nurse to special him, but once he was feeling better he would go out into the ward to provide him with some entertainment and diversions.

And that was when their real problems would start.

Adam looked up and smiled at her, then looked away, then looked back again, his eyes narrowing slightly as he scanned her face.

Oops. She hadn't got away with it. Trust him to notice. He'd spent the weekend studying her every feature. She might have realised he'd be impossible to fool.

'Sister Long,' he said quietly. 'Come and join us. You've met Mr and Mrs George, haven't you?'

'Yes, of course. How are you?' she asked the parents. 'Can I get you anything? You must have had a very trying day.'

Damian's mother smiled wanly. 'It's just so draining, waiting.'

'I know. Well, I'm going off duty now, but if you want anything, ask any of the nursing staff and they'll sort it out. Jenny will be keeping an eye on him and reporting back to Mr Bradbury, and she'll be in here with you all the time until she goes off duty at nine. There will be another nurse on for the night, and I'll be back on at seven. If there's anything you want to know, just ask one of us. OK?'

She left them with a smile, and retrieved her coat from the locker room and headed off the ward.

'Anna!'

She stopped, waiting while Adam caught up with her, and looked up into his searching eyes. 'Hi. Sorry, I thought you were busy.'

'I am. Are you all right?'

She gave him a sad smile. 'Yes, Adam, I'm all right. I'm just tired. I'm going home to bed.'

'Can I ring you? I don't want to wake you.'

'I don't mind,' she said softly. 'I don't suppose you can come round?'

He shook his head. 'Well, not until much later—about ten, and it's too late.'

'It is really,' she said reluctantly. 'You could, though, if you wanted to.'

'I'll see.' He moved away from her, back towards the ward. 'Later. Take care.'

She smiled and watched him go, then turned and made her way out of the hospital. She'd miss him if he didn't come round, but perhaps it would be better if he didn't. As Josh had said, it was too much, too soon, and she maybe needed time to come to terms with it all.

Adam got as far as his car, then thought better of it. Be rational, he told himself. You can't spend every minute of every night with her, and then work all day. It's just silly.

He locked the car again and trudged back inside, hung up his coat, poured a small glass of Scotch and went up to his room. There he kicked off his shoes, settled himself on the bed and picked up the phone.

'Hi,' he said in answer to her hello. 'Are you all right?'

'Mmm. I was asleep. It's lovely to hear your voice.'

'Are you in bed?' he asked, and felt the longing ache begin.

'Mmm. I miss you. It seems odd without you here now.'

He closed his eyes and groaned softly. 'Anna, don't,' he murmured. 'I was coming over.'

'You should have.'

'No. We need sleep. Anyway, I've got a drink now, I can't drive.'

'Oh.' Was it his imagination, or did she sound disappointed?

'Are you really OK?' he asked again, still concerned about her. He was sure she'd been crying, but he couldn't imagine why. Surely she and Josh—

'You and Josh,' he said abruptly. 'You don't have a thing going, do you?'

Her laughter nearly cut through his eardrum. 'Josh? Are you kidding? He's got a gorgeous wife he'd kill for, and two beautiful little children, a boy and a girl. There's no way he'd look at another woman.'

'What about you?' he asked, trying to keep the acid burn of jealousy in check.

She hesitated for a moment, and when she spoke there was a note of reproach in her voice that made him ashamed. 'What about me, Adam? Didn't the weekend convince you? I don't have a thing going with anyone—only you.'

'I'm sorry. I didn't mean to sound like that. I just wondered... You seemed upset after you talked to him. I didn't know why.'

She sighed softly, and he wished he'd gone round there, that they were having this conversation face to face, so he could read her beautiful expressive eyes.

'I just got upset—he asked about you. He thinks

it's too sudden. He behaves like a big brother with us all. It's nothing. You learn to ignore it after a while.'

Big brother? He had an overwhelming urge to push Josh Lancaster's teeth down his interfering throat. How *dare* he presume to tell Anna off for her relationship with him?

'Hey, stop it, I can feel you getting angry,' Anna said in gentle reproach. 'He means well. He's very kind.'

Adam didn't want to talk about him any more. He didn't want to talk, full stop. He wanted to hold her, and touch her, and watch her fall apart under his hands. He looked at the untouched Scotch in the glass, and wondered if he had any self-control at all.

Then he heard Jaz cry out in his sleep, and with a sigh he picked up the glass and drained it.

That would fix it. He couldn't go to her now. He didn't ever drink and drive, not after what he'd seen in A and E. 'I have to go,' he said reluctantly. 'Jasper's crying, he needs me. I'll see you tomorrow. Sleep well.'

'You, too. Hope he's all right.'

'He'll be fine. 'Night, Anna. Take care.'

He put the phone down very carefully, swung his legs over the edge of the bed and padded softly next door. Danny was asleep in his bed behind the door, and Jasper was sitting up on the far side, knuckling his eyes and sobbing quietly.

'It's all right, Jaz, I'm here,' he murmured reassuringly. Scooping the little lad up, he sat on his bed and cradled him against his chest.

'Had a dream,' Jaz hiccuped unhappily. 'I was f'ightened.'

'It's all gone now,' Adam assured him. 'You're safe now, I've got you.'

And if I'd gone to Anna, I wouldn't have been here for him, and Helle wouldn't have heard him over her music.

Suddenly his burning desire to be with Anna was extinguished, replaced by the need to nurture and care for his children, and shelter them from the fears and perils of their hitherto insecure little lives.

'It's all right,' he said again, rocking him until the little body relaxed against him and was still. Then he slid Jaz under the covers, tucked him up and went to bed, trying not to think of Anna and how big and empty his kingsize bed felt after sharing her much smaller one all weekend.

He couldn't abandon his responsibilities, and he didn't want to. What he wanted, what he needed, was a retreat, somewhere he could run to and hide when it all got too much. An oasis of calm and warmth and tenderness, a place to go to recharge his batteries and refill his soul.

He thought of Anna and her gentleness, and her peace seemed to steal over him.

'Goodnight, my love,' he whispered softly. 'Sleep tight.'

Two miles away, Anna lay in bed with her hands wrapped around a scarf Adam had left there. It was soft and cosy, and it carried the faint tang of his aftershave. She cradled it under her chin, and thought of him, and ached for him. She felt his presence with her somehow, almost as if he was thinking of her. Was he in bed already? Hers seemed awfully empty without him. Empty and cold.

*Goodnight, my love. Sleep tight.*

She snuggled the scarf closer, inhaling deeply and focusing on him in his huge bed in that enormous, empty bedroom.

'Goodnight, my love,' she whispered in the silent room. 'Sleep tight. See you tomorrow.'

She seemed to feel his arms around her, holding her, his warmth stealing over her, and within moments she was asleep.

# CHAPTER SIX

'DAMIAN, we're going to turn you,' Anna said gently. 'All right?'

'No-o-o,' the boy protested, his voice barely audible. 'Please, no.'

'Sorry, sweetheart. I'll give you a bit more pain relief, OK?'

'Does it hurt him very much?' his mother asked, looking troubled.

'Probably a bit,' Anna told her as she overrode the syringe driver and gave him a little more of the drug. 'It's also quite scary. When I was training we had to lie in it and be turned so we knew what it was like, and it's a bit unnerving. It squashes you a bit with both halves on and, although you're pretty stable inside it, you do feel a bit vulnerable. I can quite understand why he doesn't like it, but he'd hate being turned any other way much, much more, believe me.'

Anna and Jenny clipped the other half of the revolving bed-frame on top of him, fastened it securely so that he was firmly sandwiched between the layers, and then turned it over, so that he went from his back to his front, with his face cradled in a special cut-out.

He whimpered as they turned it, but it had to be done, and once the upper piece of frame was removed they soon made him comfortable again.

Anna left the dressing until Adam arrived. She was sure he'd be in early to check up on Damian and Kate before going to his clinic, and she was right. He appeared shortly before eight, and she left Allie taking report and joined him just outside Damian's room.

Adam gave her a brief but intimate smile of greeting and moved a little further away from the door so they were no longer in earshot. 'Morning. How's my favourite nurse today?' he murmured.

'Busy—how are you?'

'Ditto. I've got a clinic in a minute. How's he been in the night?'

'All right, I think. He hates being turned over.'

'I'm sure he does. I expect it hurts. Use the override on the syringe driver a few minutes before to give him a bit of extra pain relief,' he suggested.

'We do. It still hurts.'

'Hmm. Well, there's nothing else we can do, he's on the most we can really give him. It'll get better. Today will be the worst, I expect. Can I have a look at the wound?'

'Sure. I've got the trolley ready. I was waiting for you.'

'Thanks.' His smile warmed her down to her toes, and she knew it was nothing to do with Damian and everything to do with their conversation last night. 'Anna?'

She paused on the threshold of the room.

'I missed you last night,' he said, so softly she could hardly hear him.

'Ditto,' she replied just as softly. 'It was a long night.'

'What time do you have lunch?'

She laughed under her breath. 'If and when I can get away, usually. Why don't you ring me when you're free?'

'Good idea. Right, let's see how Damian's getting on.'

'Are you OK?'

Anna looked up from her paperwork to see Josh leaning over the top of the work station, his arms propped on the high, narrow counter.

She gave him a forgiving smile. 'Yes, I'm fine, thanks.'

'I hear interesting things about your Mr Bradbury,' he murmured. 'I gather he's pretty top-flight.'

'So I'm told.' It didn't surprise her. She imagined he was the sort of man who was good at everything he did, and if his love-making was anything to go by, he was a stickler for detail.

'Robert Ryder was impressed. He assisted with a case on Friday night, apparently, and saved a leg anyone else would have given up on. Apparently, the young woman is doing well, despite having lost the other leg and her fiancé in the crash.'

So that was what he'd been doing. She'd wondered what it had been that had put that haunted look in his eyes. 'I don't know how anybody can bear to do orthopaedics,' she said with a shudder. 'The trauma side is so messy.'

'A and E is what gets me. You get the lot. I really, really don't like blood.' He grinned. 'So what have you got for me?'

'Oh, hundreds of new admissions,' she teased. The phone rang, and she scooped it up.

'Children's ward, Sister Long speaking. Can I help you?'

'Lunch?'

She glanced at her watch. 'Can you give me five minutes?'

'Sure. I'll meet you in the Gallery.'

'OK.'

She cradled the phone and looked up at Josh. 'Right. Allie will show you your new cases. There are only two. One's got some kind of flu that won't shift and is turning into what looks like pneumonia, the other looks like diabetes.'

'Thanks. I'll go and see them. You go and have lunch with your maestro.'

She coloured. 'What makes you think—?'

'Don't bother,' he said with a lazy grin. 'It's written all over your face in letters ten feet high.'

'My face isn't that big.'

'Your smile is.'

She laughed and stood up. 'Are you going to watch my every movement?'

'No—actually, I'm hoping to sell you tickets for the Valentine Ball on Saturday night. It's a fundraiser for the children's facilities in the department. You have a moral duty to support it. We've got a couple of spaces on our table—why don't you join us?'

'I'll ask him,' she promised, her heart thumping at the thought of spending the evening dancing with Adam. 'I'll let you know.'

She all but ran through the hospital, and found him sitting at a table in the Gallery coffee-shop. It was the nearest to the paediatric ward, and served snacks and drinks. Hardly lunching out, but it was quick, and that was all she had time for.

Adam stood up and came towards her, ushering her to the counter. 'You took six minutes,' he said in mock reproof, and she glanced at her watch.

'Did I?'

He laughed. 'I have no idea. It just seemed like a long time. What are you going to eat?'

She shrugged. 'I don't know. A sandwich?'

'Good idea.'

They took their selection out of the chiller, added mugs of coffee to the tray and he paid for it and led her back to the table where he'd been sitting.

'I'm starving,' she confessed, biting into her sandwich enthusiastically.

'Must be all that activity at the weekend,' he teased gently, and she felt herself colour a little.

'It seems a long time ago,' she said wistfully, picking out a prawn.

'Too long. What are you doing tonight?'

She looked up into his eyes, and read the unmistakable invitation in them. 'Waiting up for you?' she suggested, and he gave a crooked, sexy smile that made her heart flutter.

'Sounds good.'

'This weekend,' she said, trying not to drown in his eyes, 'there's a Valentine Ball in aid of the hospital children's facilities. Josh asked if we wanted to join their table. I said I'd ask you.'

He looked thoughtful. 'A Valentine Ball? I haven't danced for years. Have you got strong shoes?'

She chuckled. 'No—little strappy, open-toed ones—and I warn you, I love dancing, so you'd better be good at it.'

'I'll do,' he confessed, and searched her eyes. 'Fancy it?'

She nodded. 'I do, actually. I haven't been to a ball for ages, and I love to party.'

'OK, Cinderella,' he said with a lazy, sexy smile,

'you shall go to the ball. Just don't turn into a pumpkin at midnight.'

'That was the coach,' she laughed, and he grinned.

'So it was. My mistake. What time tonight?'

Tonight. Her heart slammed against her ribs. 'Whenever. What time can you make it?'

He shrugged. 'Depends on the kids. I can't stay long. Last night Jasper woke up crying and needed a cuddle—I'd hate to think I wasn't there for him.'

'What does he do when you're at work?'

'He cries, I suppose,' Adam said heavily. 'I don't know. I try not to think about it.'

'They need a mother,' she said, her heart aching at the thought of Jasper lying crying in his bed, all alone. 'Poor little loves.'

'No,' he said with quiet certainty, and a chill ran over her. 'No, Anna, they don't need a mother, and I don't need a wife. Don't start thinking along those lines, please. I need you, yes—God knows I need you—but not as a wife. Not as a mother for my children. Been there, done that. It was a disaster. No, our relationship's going nowhere, Anna, except where it is—a beautiful little oasis of calm and tranquillity in the midst of my chaotic existence. I'm sorry if that's not what you see for us, but it's all I can give you—all I can ask of you. I'm sorry.'

She dropped her eyes, unwilling to let him see the pain she knew must be all too obvious in them. You're wrong! she wanted to shout. Of course you need a wife!

But perhaps he didn't. Perhaps he was right. She sat there, chasing bubbles in her coffee with the spoon, and swallowed the hurt before she made a complete ass of herself.

'Anna?' His voice was kind, and he placed gentle fingers under her chin and tilted her head so he could see into her tear-filled eyes. 'Damn,' he said softly, and brushed a tear away with his thumb. 'Oh, sweetheart, don't cry. I didn't say I don't need you. I do—probably more than you can imagine.'

He glanced around, sighed and dropped his hand. 'We can't talk about this here. I'll come round tonight—*may* I come round tonight?'

She closed her eyes and looked away. 'I don't know. Yes, of course you can come round.' She gave a tremulous sigh and met his eyes again. 'Of course you can. I'll see you later.'

She stood up and brushed the crumbs off her tabard, then without another word she left him there, went into the nearest ladies' loo and shut herself in, flushing it to drown out the sobs that wouldn't be suppressed.

Give him time, she told herself, blowing her nose and scrubbing tears from her cheeks. Give him time.

She washed her face, patted it dry, dug in her pocket for her rescue kit and went back to the ward, patched up and ready to go.

'Hell, again?' Josh said, cornering her in the kitchen. 'What now?'

'He doesn't need a wife.'

Josh smiled. 'Good. He's thinking about it.'

'No. I said his children need a mother. *I'm* thinking about it, not him. He put me right.'

Josh let out his breath on a harsh sigh. 'So you won't be joining us for the ball, then?'

His bleeper squawked, and he went into the office to use the phone. He came back a moment later, a wry smile on his face. 'Curious. That was Adam—he asked if I'd got the ball tickets. He'd like to buy two. Apparently, he's under the illusion that you'll still go with him.'

Her humourless little laugh was cut off in its prime. 'Oh, I will—he's right. I can't refuse him anything. I love him, Josh, and he needs me. That's the long and the short of it. I love him, and I'll take any crumbs he throws me—and that's all he can spare. Crumbs...' Her voice cracked on the word, and she bit her lip and turned away.

'Hey, hey, don't be so pessimistic,' Josh said encouragingly. 'Lots of people fight shy of commitment, especially if they've been burned before. If he says he needs you, Anna, he'll relent in the end. Take my word for it. You hang in there and make yourself indispensable to him. He'll come round. Lissa did. You just have to wait him out. Withhold privileges or something,' he suggested, laughter in his voice.

'I can't be so calculated,' she protested. 'And anyway, I need him, too.' She let out a soft sigh. 'I know I'm going to get hurt, whatever happens, but I can't walk away.'

'I'm sorry,' he said gently, and laid a kindly hand on her arm. 'Look, if you need a shoulder to cry on, you know where we are, any time, day or night. Just come round. Lissa's there most of the day, and we're always in in the evening. You know you're welcome.'

She dredged up a smile. 'Thanks, Josh. You're a good friend.'

'Any time.'

She went out into the ward and found Allie, and her friend shot her a searching look.

'Don't ask,' she warned. 'Please.'

'Oh, Anna! Come on, you need to be busy,' she

said briskly. 'Damian needs turning—want to give me a hand? And then we need to check the dressing on Kate's leg.'

Together they turned Damian again and made him comfortable, and then went to see Kate, who was just starting the leg-lengthening procedure.

She was in a little pain, but she seemed relieved that the operation was over and the real business of stretching out the short leg could begin. Adam had showed her how to turn the key, and how far, and she would be doing it herself, an important part of the process.

The wounds looked clean and healthy, and Anna was impressed at the neatness of the incision and the almost invisible stitching. It would heal beautifully, she realised. Just another of Adam's many skills.

Then she checked the little girl with pneumonia and made sure she was comfortable and breathing as well as she could. She was being monitored frequently, and her vital signs had been improving over the last hour or so that she had been in.

'Dr Lancaster's ever so kind, isn't he?' the child's mother said, and Anna agreed.

He was kind. Kind and thoughtful, and he'd moved heaven and earth to convince Lissa to marry him when she'd been expecting their first child. When he talked about patience, he was at least talking from a standpoint of personal experience. Perhaps he was right.

And perhaps pigs flew.

The doorbell rang at a quarter to ten, and Anna opened it to find Adam there, flowers in his hand and regret in his eyes. 'Can I come in?'

'Of course you can. I said that.'

He put the flowers down, and drew her into his arms. 'I'm sorry I hurt you,' he murmured. 'I just didn't want you building up unrealistic dreams. I'm sorry if I was too late.'

You were too late the moment I first saw you, Anna thought, and hugged him gently back. 'Don't be silly. Do you want a drink?'

He shook his head. 'No. I just want you.'

Without a word she turned and led the way upstairs.

It was strange, the rest of that week. She was looking forward to the ball, but she was too busy to think about it much, and Saturday was rushing up like an express train.

'Have you got a dress?' Allie asked on Friday, and she nodded.

'A strappy cream thing—it's quite slinky and it's split all the way up to wherever, but it suits me and I own it and I don't have time to go shopping.'

Allie laughed and shook her head. 'You ought to spoil yourself. Don't you want to impress him?'

Pain stabbed her. 'I don't think a dress will do it,' she said drily. 'Come and give me a hand with Damian. I want to move him out into the ward. He's bored and fractious, and I think he might be better with something to look at and someone to talk to. We'll need to do something ingenious with mirrors so he can see the television, but I'm sure we can cheer him up.'

They were just moving him into his new position when her senses went on red alert. She lifted her head, and Adam was standing in the entrance to the ward, watching her. He was too far away for her to see his expression, but she had known he was there. How strange, and yet not strange at all. She felt she knew everything about him. Why would she not know when he was near?

He came towards her, every step echoing her heartbeat, and a fleeting smile quirked his lips. 'Hello, all. Hi, Damian. How are things?'

'Boring,' the boy said.

'We're moving him so there's more to see and do,' Anna explained. 'We're going to rig up mirrors so he can see round the ward, and watch the television and so on.'

'That should make things better for you, Damian. Good—' He turned to Anna. 'Could I have a word, Sister, please?'

'Of course.' She left Damian in Allie's capable hands and followed Adam into the vacated side room. 'What is it?'

'Apart from the fact that I just wanted to see you?' he said with a wry smile. 'I've got a six-year-old child with osteogenesis imperfecta who's just moved into the area recently and is supposedly coming in for correction of bowing and multiple fractures of both femurs. She's very small—tiny for her age, no bigger than a toddler—and she's very frail. She's got a pigeon chest and scoliosis, and very limited limb growth. I don't know what I can do for her, I suspect not a lot, but she's fallen and broken her arm and leg this morning and she's coming up in a minute.'

'Are you going to pin and plate her?'

He shrugged. 'I don't know. I can't decide. I have to say I'm not very hopeful. I think she's too fragile to treat except very conservatively, and I'm wary of going in and doing more damage. There's nothing to screw anything to, it's all too fragile, and really I don't know how she's survived so far. I've never seen such brittle bones.

'It's a collagen problem, of course, and the brittle bones are just a symptom, so I think we might try to treat the collagen deficiency long term, but for now we might have to put her in a very lightweight cast so, please, make sure the nursing staff know how fragile she is.'

'I will,' Anna promised, wondering how they would manage her. 'She'll need a Propad mattress and sheepskin. I'll see to that. She'll need a cot as well, I think—I don't want to risk her falling out of bed. We'd better pad the bars. Is her mother coming with her?'

'Yes. She's the one that's got her through so far, so I would use her whenever possible. She's used to handling her and they have a system, apparently. I have to say, I think we might lose her. She's really brave apparently, but, of course, every fracture hurts as much as another, and just because it happens to her all the time that doesn't mean it isn't painful.'

Adam sighed and ran his hands through his hair. 'I thought I had some time this afternoon to catch up on my paperwork, but it doesn't look like it now. She's come to the top of the list in a major way, but I don't think I'll do a lot before Monday. I'll come and see her once you've got her settled and I'll decide then. I'll go and have another look at the pictures and see what I think. I might ring an old colleague.'

He was just leaving the room when he turned back. 'Still all right for tomorrow?'

'I am—what about you?'

He closed his eyes and grunted with laughter. 'Helle can't babysit. She's going to London again. My parents have said they'll come and stay—that means I'll get the third degree if I stay out after midnight.'

'Really?'

He laughed again. 'Maybe. I don't know. I haven't tried. Knowing my mother, she'd be delighted to know there was a woman in my life. She's insatiably curious as it is. She knows I'm taking someone to the ball, she just doesn't know who—and she certainly doesn't know we're having an affair. She'd be over the moon. She thinks I'm a recluse.'

No, just a lonely, generous man who'd given his heart to his children and sworn to protect them no matter what the cost.

'We'll just have to go home early, then,' Anna said with a smile, and his eyes darkened fractionally.

'Promises, promises,' he murmured, and walked away, whistling softly.

'You look stunning.'

Anna laughed and stroked Adam's satin lapel. 'You don't look so bad yourself. I like the bow-tie—very professional.'

'And it's real,' he told her smugly. 'None of your elasticated nonsense.'

He helped her into her coat, dropped a quick, hard kiss on her lips and then had to wait while she wiped the lipstick off his mouth with a tissue.

'Why did you do that?' he asked. 'I thought I'd set a trend.'

'Very fetching. It's not your colour. You'd look better in plum.'

'I'll bear it in mind.'

It was only a short drive to the hotel where the ball was being held, and it was moments before they'd handed over their coats and were inside, surrounded by red roses, silver hearts and romantic music.

'St Valentine, eat your heart out,' Adam said softly in her ear. 'Right, where are the others? Do we need to meet up with them?'

'Over there—I can see Josh waving. They're all there.' And, please, she thought, don't let Josh grill him about his intentions or let on that he knows anything. Anything at all!

He didn't. He stood up to greet them, and said, 'I expect you know most of us. This is my wife, Lissa, and Sarah Jordan, Matt's wife, from A and E, and you know Matt and Mark and Allie already. We're still waiting for Nick and Ronnie Sarazin—they might be late. One of the children was ill, apparently. Now, can I get you two a drink? I'm just going up to the bar.'

The meal was wonderful, and as they lingered over coffee the master of ceremonies called for everyone's attention, thanked them for supporting the cause and ordered them to dance. The band struck up, and Adam turned to Anna with a challenging smile.

'You wanted to party,' he said slowly. 'Let's party.'

She returned his smile, stood up and took his hand. 'Excuse us, folks. We're here to dance.'

She followed him onto the empty floor and went into his arms. It was a pacy number, with a heavy beat, and he slotted one thigh between hers, laid a guiding hand on the small of her back and led her in an intricate series of swoops and swirls that left her laughing and breathless and everyone clapping.

It was followed by another, and another, with everyone joining in, and then the band slowed down and he locked his arms behind her back and smiled down at her. 'Enjoying yourself?' he asked.

'Absolutely. You're an exhibitionist,' she said in amazement, and he laughed. 'And a liar,' she added. 'You didn't tread on my toes once!'

'Ah. I asked if you had strong shoes—I didn't say I was going to tread on you! You're pretty special, you know that? You didn't miss a single beat.'

'Nor did you. I'm stunned. So many men have two left feet.'

'Ah, well, you know what they say about good dancers.'

She tried to stifle a smile. 'If you're fishing for compliments on your technique in other areas, you can fish,' she teased.

'You're a hard woman.'

'I wouldn't want you to get a swollen head.'

'No danger of that. I'm sure you wouldn't allow it for a moment.' He drew her closer and sighed in her ear. 'You smell good,' he murmured.

'So do you. I could breathe you in all night.'

'Not a chance. I think Josh is back with our drinks, and I'm gasping after that lot,' he said, and eased away from her with reluctance. 'Shall we go back to the table?'

'We ought to, or they'll complain that we're being antisocial.'

Needless to say, they were teased about the dancing.

'Very sexy,' Lissa said, eyeing them with interest.

'Tell me, were you actually screwed together, or was that just an illusion?'

'Lissa!' Josh exclaimed, and everyone laughed aloud.

'Just an illusion,' Adam assured her with a smile.

'I just wondered if, being an orthopaedic surgeon, you could lend a whole new meaning to the term "joined at the hip".' She turned to her husband and eyed him speculatively. 'Josh, can you dance like that?'

'Not in public,' he said reprovingly, and Anna laughed, still on a high from the best dance she'd had in years.

'You're just a stuffed shirt. Your wife wants to dance, Josh, take her up on it. You might not get a better offer all night.'

'Later. I need to get a bit more tanked up before I make an ass of myself.'

They all laughed, and the conversation settled down and became more general. Adam was asked about his house, and he told them about the general state of it and the vast amount of decorating that needed to be done.

'You ought to have a stripping party,' Lissa suggested. 'They're always lots of fun.'

Everyone laughed, and Adam shook his head. 'I'd worry about your wife, if I were you, Josh,' he said with a chuckle. 'I think you've got your hands full there.'

'Wallpaper,' Lissa said firmly, trying not to laugh. 'You get everyone round and hire wallpaper strippers and get loads of food in and, Bob's your uncle, it's all stripped. Fun. We'll come.'

'You haven't been invited yet,' Josh reminded her, and she rolled her eyes.

'I'll have you know I'm a dab hand with a wall-paper stripper,' she said proudly.

'I'll think about it,' Adam promised. 'And now, if you'll excuse us, I'm going to take Anna back to the dance floor and find out what else she can do.'

'This I have to see,' Mark said with a chuckle. 'You've been hiding your light under a bushel, Anna.'

'You've all had your chance,' she reminded them. 'It's not my fault you didn't know a good thing when you saw it.'

'Stop flirting with them, they're all taken,' Adam said, towing her to her feet. 'Come on, woman, I want your body. The night's awasting.'

It couldn't get any better, she thought, but she was wrong. They danced together, they danced apart, they danced around each other, they jived, they tangoed, they waltzed, and then finally, with the last and most romantic number to wind up a valentine ball, they stood almost still and swayed against each other.

Anna thought she'd never been so in tune with any-one or so aware of them in her life. She rested her head on Adam's shoulder, her arms round his waist under his jacket, and wished the evening didn't have to come to an end.

Finally, though, it was time to go, and they said goodnight to the others and walked back to the car, his arm slung round her shoulders, their hips bumping with every stride. It was a cold, crisp night, but they were warm from the dancing and still running on adrenaline, so they hardly noticed.

He parked outside her house and cut the engine, then took the keys from her and opened her front door, closing it behind them and drawing her back into his arms.

'Where were we?' he asked gruffly, and slid her coat over her shoulders. His own followed it to the floor, then he kicked off his shoes, shucked off his jacket, tugged the bow-tie loose and slid the cuff-links free.

Anna turned and walked towards the stairs, kicking off her shoes as she went, and he followed her, catching her by the ankle and placing a kiss in the centre of her foot.

She laughed and pulled it away, turning round and watching as he stripped off his shirt and dropped it on the hall floor. The trousers followed, and the socks, leaving him in nothing but wholly inadequate briefs. She backed up the stairs, trapped by the fever in his eyes, and went into the bedroom.

She'd set the scene tonight, placing candles on the chest of drawers, putting fresh linen on the bed, his flowers in a vase on the dressing table. It probably gave away too much, but she didn't care. She was no good at hiding things, she never had been, and he might as well know the truth.

She lit the candles, and while she stooped over them, Adam bent and laid his lips against the bare, heated skin of her shoulders. 'You're beautiful,' he murmured, sliding down the zip on her dress and easing the fine spaghetti straps off the shoulders.

It puddled round her ankles, leaving her dressed in nothing more than a pair of slinky tights, and he slid his hands round from behind her and cupped her breasts, their reflection in the mirror pearly in the candlelight.

'Beautiful,' he said again, and turned her into his

arms. His kiss was tender, slow and lazy, belying the heat that raged between them.

Or maybe not. A shudder ran through him, and he lifted his head and looked deep into her eyes, his own filled with fire.

'I want you,' he said, his voice uneven. 'Make love with me, Anna. I need you.'

Adam's honesty tore through her, and her arms wrapped around him and held him close to her heart. His head dropped against her shoulder, his lips pressed firmly against the soft skin of her throat, and he stood there for several seconds without moving. Then he lifted his head and gave her a crooked little smile.

'We've got a dance to finish,' he murmured, and peeled the gossamer tights away. He lifted her and laid her in the middle of the bed, and then he kissed her, every inch of her, his touch gentle and reverent, until she wanted to weep with longing.

Finally, when she thought she'd die without him, he moved over her, his body trembling under her hands, and then he hesitated, poised over her, their eyes locked.

'I love you,' he said softly, and then her body welcomed him, and she knew she could never love anyone more than she loved this man…

# CHAPTER SEVEN

'I HAVE to go.'

Anna opened her eyes and looked up into Adam's sombre face. His eyes were troubled. 'I know,' she murmured.

'I'm sorry. You know I'd stay if I could.'

She nodded. 'It's all right, I do understand.'

He kissed her, then levered himself up and swung his legs over the side of the bed.

She watched him as he stood up and walked to the door, retrieving his briefs on the way. 'I have no idea where my clothes are,' he said with a wry grin.

'Just follow the trail,' she suggested, and blew him a kiss.

A few minutes later he reappeared, dressed, and came and sat on the edge of the bed. 'I think I've found everything,' he said. His eyes were still shadowed with regret. His head descended slowly, blocking out the mellow, golden glow of the candles, and his mouth touched hers. 'I'll see you on Monday morning. Look after yourself.'

'You, too.'

He ran lightly down the stairs, and then a moment later she heard the front door closing, then the sound of his car starting outside in the street. She looked at the bedside clock. It was three-fifteen. They'd been home less than two hours.

She told herself she was being greedy, wanting more of him, but she missed him already. She lay down with her head where his had rested on the pillow and breathed deeply, inhaling the faint scent of his aftershave and something more individual, something just Adam.

Her arms felt empty, but her heart was full. He loved her. He'd said so. That must surely be progress?

She curled up on her side, tugging the quilt round her to keep her warm, and eventually she fell asleep.

When she woke, the candles had burned right down, and the sun was shining through the crack in the curtains. She looked at her watch. Nine-thirty. Only six hours' sleep, and yet she felt wonderful. She threw off the quilt, pulled on her robe and went downstairs, picking up the trail of discarded clothing as she went.

Her toe hit something, and she looked down to see a small leather wallet on the floor. Adam's. She bent and picked it up, hefting it in her hand. He'd need it today—he might go and fill the car up with petrol and then realise he didn't have it, or spend hours searching for it.

She'd take it round. It was no trouble, and it was a good excuse to see him again. She took a cup of tea with her to the bath, drank it while she soaked in the lovely hot water and then washed and dressed in record time.

She left the house by ten, and arrived at Adam's shortly afterwards. His car was the only one on the drive, so she turned in there and pulled up beside it. His parents must have gone. Good. She didn't need an inquisition this morning, and she was sure he didn't either.

She hoped he was up. She tipped her head back and looked at the windows, and saw his curtains open.

Good. She didn't want to wake him if they were all still asleep, but she didn't think it was likely. Children woke up revoltingly early, on the whole.

She rang the doorbell, listening to it echoing down the hall, and a moment later the door swung open to reveal an elegant, grey-haired woman in her sixties. His mother. It must be. Oh, yipes. She thought they'd gone, as the car wasn't there. She'd just assumed—

'Can I help you, dear?' the woman asked, and she conjured up a smile.

'Yes. Is Adam in?'

'He is—he's in the garden with the children, building a bonfire. Hold on, I'll get him.'

She was about to turn away when Anna stopped her. 'It's all right—I've got his wallet. He dropped it in my house last night. Perhaps you could just give it to him?'

The woman searched her face slowly, then smiled. 'You must be Anna—come in, dear. Give it to him yourself, I'm sure he'll be pleased to see you. I've just made a big pot of tea, actually. Perhaps you'll join us, or are you a coffee person?'

Anna found herself in the kitchen, clutching a couple of mugs and being ushered toward the table. 'Sit down, I'll get him. Adam? Adam, it's for you. Anna.'

He came in, and did a mild double take. 'Hi—I thought you were on the phone.'

'You dropped your wallet,' she said, suddenly feeling guilty for allowing his mother to talk her into staying. 'In the hall. I thought you'd want it. Your mother gave me a cup of tea.'

'I can imagine,' he said drily, and gave a wry grin. 'Thanks for bringing my wallet round. It was good of you. I would have missed it later.'

Adam hooked a chair out with his foot and sat down, cradling the mug in his hands. 'I was just telling my father about Lissa's stripping party,' he said, not looking at all worried that she was there, ensconced uninvited in his breakfast room. 'Do you think anyone would come?'

'Oh, yes,' Anna said instantly. 'I'm sure they would, just out of curiosity. It's a sort of alternative house-warming, isn't it?'

He laughed. 'I suppose so—very alternative. I hardly know most of these people, though. Why would they bother?'

'Because they're nice? Because they like doing things to help and to make people welcome? Because they'll do anything for a free meal? When were you thinking of?'

He gave a short laugh. 'I wasn't, really. It sounds like bedlam. I'm not sure I can stand more than one room at a time in chaos.'

Anna looked round her and raised an eyebrow. 'Nothing on the walls is better than what's there now—but you might need a crack-filling party to follow it!'

'Don't.'

His mother entered the room behind him, trying hard to look casual and failing dismally. 'Biscuit, anyone?'

'No, thanks, I've only just had breakfast. Anna?'

'I'd love one. I sort of forgot breakfast today.' In my haste to get here. Oh, dear.

'I'll get them. More tea, Anna? Adam, do you want a top-up, darling?'

'No, thanks,' they said together, and their eyes locked and they smiled.

'Stay for lunch,' he said impulsively, and so she did, and they planned the stripping party, and finished building the bonfire, and before they knew what was going on it was night-time and she had to go.

'Thank you for today,' she said as he saw her off at the door. They were in the porch, in the space between the inner and outer doors, and although the doors had stained glass in them, the light in the porch wasn't on and so they had an element of privacy.

'It's been a pleasure,' he said, and, as if he couldn't help himself, he lowered his head and kissed her. It was only a brief kiss, but there was enough heat bottled up in it to keep her warm all the way home.

What had he been thinking about, asking Anna for lunch? She'd stayed all day, and it had been torture. He'd wanted to hold her, and touch her, and his mother's eagle eyes had missed nothing.

Neither had the children's, and in the bath after she'd gone the boys were grilling him.

'She's nice—why can't she come and live with us instead of Helle?'

'Yes, why can't she? I don't like Helle.'

'Yes, you do, Jasper,' Adam said firmly, taking a flannel and scrubbing it over his grubby little hands.

'I don't. She's not as nice as Anna.'

Adam had to agree privately, but it didn't make his life any easier. 'She's got a job,' he told them, going back to the original issue while he lathered. 'She can't come and work for us.'

'She could just stay.'

'She's got a house.'

'We've got a house. I bet her house isn't as big as our house.'

No, Adam thought, but it's warm and cosy and it's a peaceful haven compared to this. He lifted Jasper out of the bath, wrapped him in a towel and gave Danny a helping hand out.

'You could ask her,' Danny persisted. 'I bet you haven't asked her.'

'No, I haven't and, what's more, I'm not going to. Helle's going anyway, remember, and we're getting another au pair. She's coming soon.'

Not soon enough, though. Helle was starting to drive him mad. She often failed to come back after the weekend—like this weekend, for instance. She would probably turn up at eight tomorrow morning, after he wanted to be at the hospital, and it would be a logistical nightmare.

He'd probably have to take the children round to his parents and leave them to drop them at school—which meant getting them up early, getting their snacks organised, finding all the things for their school bags. It was hell, and all because Helle couldn't be bothered to come back when she was supposed to.

'Skye?' he called, sticking his head out of the bathroom door. 'Your turn, darling.'

'Coming.'

He pulled Jasper's pyjama top on over his head, cleaned his teeth, trundled him into the loo next door for a last visit and returned to Danny who was just rinsing out the toothpaste. 'What about your hair? Want me to rub it dry?'

He stood in front of Adam obediently, allowing him to towel it. Then, when it was dry enough for the night, he looked Adam straight in the eye and said, without warning, 'I think you should ask her.'

'Me, too,' Jasper said, pulling up his pyjama trousers as he reappeared.

'Ask who what?' Skye said, coming into the overcrowded bathroom behind Jasper.

'Nothing. Come on, boys, let Skye have her bath in peace.'

He bundled them out of the room, went back in five minutes later and washed Skye's hair for her, then helped her dry it and combed it carefully through.

A mother's job, he thought sadly, and swallowed the lump that came out of nowhere. Damn Lyn. Damn her, damn David, damn both of them.

'Ouch!'

'Sorry, darling,' he said, instantly contrite. He had to stop himself from hugging her automatically, and instead stroked her head where he'd tugged a tangle. 'I wasn't concentrating.' He finished her hair more carefully, then rinsed round the bath and hung up the damp towels while Skye cleaned her teeth.

Ten minutes later they were all kissed and settled, and he poured himself a much-needed glass of wine and sat down in front of the television.

It couldn't hold his attention. All he could think about was Anna, and how she'd danced with him last night, and that he'd told her he loved her.

He hadn't meant to do that. He'd meant to keep it to himself, but he'd fouled up. She'd looked so lovely, her face delicately flushed with passion, her eyes soft, her touch so tender—it had cut through his defences, and dragged the truth from him. She'd deserved the truth, and he'd given it to her, but she deserved more than that.

She deserved the follow-up, the next course, the icing on the cake, and he couldn't give her that.

No matter how much he might long to.

Little Emily Parker was the worst case of brittle bone disease Anna had ever seen. She'd been immobilised in casts over the weekend, but now Adam was going to try and pin her leg. If successful, he would straighten and pin the other one by cutting the bone into little pieces, rearranging them in a straight line and putting a pin through them. 'Like stringing beads on a knitting needle,' he explained to them.

'Will it be better then?' Emily asked in her curiously flat voice. She was deaf as well, from the damage to the little bones in her inner ear, and it just compounded her problems.

'I hope so,' Adam told her honestly. 'I'll do my best, and I'm good at what I do, but I can still only do what I can. I will try for you, though. I think the arm would be better in a cast, though, for now. I don't want to do too much to you at once.'

'Thank you,' her mother said. She sounded weary. No wonder, Anna thought. Emily had spent most of her six years in hospital for one thing or another, and her mother had been with her for most of it.

She and Adam left Emily's cot, and went back into the office. 'Are you OK?' she asked him, looking into his tired eyes. 'You look a bit harassed this morning.'

'Helle didn't come back from her weekend. She's back now—I just got her on the phone. I gave her hell. I expect she'll have packed and gone by the time I get home. Oh, well. So be it. I must contact a nanny agency. The au pair people are taking for ever and I need some cover.'

'What about the girls next door? Can they help out?' Anna suggested.

'Well, they can babysit occasionally, but not much more than that. I have to do something permanent—it's no good going on like this. Helle's just not reliable enough, and neither was the last one.'

He looked at his watch and sighed. 'I suppose I ought to go and scrub and start my list. I've got the two-year-old with spina bifida for closure of the spinal tract, and little Emily, and the two fractures that have come in overnight that need my attention. I'll see you later—are you in tonight?'

She would have cancelled almost anything. As it was, there was nothing to cancel. 'Yes, I'm free,' she told him. 'Come round, if you've still got an au pair.'

He snorted softly. 'On second thoughts, don't hold your breath. I might ring you instead.'

He did, to tell her that Helle had still been there when he'd got home, but was only going to work the week.

'What about the phone bill?' Anna asked, knowing how soft he was. 'Are you going to hold her to that?'

'I don't suppose so,' he admitted. 'It was an attempt to persuade her to stay for a while, but it's not been very effective. I've tried an agency, but they can't do anything before next week at the earliest.'

'If I can help at all, just ask me,' Anna offered, but he didn't take her up on it. Still, the offer had been made. 'How was the op on Emily?' she asked. 'I had to leave before you came back to the ward.'

'OK. Not as bad as I thought. I did both legs, and I left her arm in a cast. I just hope the ends of the bone are strong enough to stand the strain. That's the danger, of course. Still, there's only so much I can do. The spinal tract case was easier than I thought, but one of the fractures was a monster. You'll meet him tomorrow—he'll be with us for a while. How was Damian today?'

'Bored,' she said with a smile that he must have heard in her voice. 'I've got a girl in on work experience who wants to be a doctor—I'm going to get her to entertain him and find ways of making his life more interesting. It should help her make up her mind one way or the other.'

Adam chuckled, a low, sexy sound that unsettled her, and she shifted her position on the bed and wished he was there with her.

They talked for nearly another hour, saying nothing much, just enjoying the sound of each other's voices, and then finally he sighed. 'I have to go. I can hear one of the boys up. I'll see you tomorrow. Think of me while you curl up all alone in your bed.'

Hah! As if she needed telling! She lay back against the pillows and sighed softly. Give him time, she said to herself for the millionth time. He'll come round. Josh said so.

Josh was an expert in persuasion. He'd moved his caravan onto Lissa's drive and camped outside her house when she'd been pregnant with their first baby. Eventually she'd surrendered. Maybe Adam would give in, too, if she waited long enough.

'Whose idea was this?' Adam asked himself, standing in the middle of the hall while his house was systematically stripped from floor to ceiling. The boys' room, Skye's room and the sitting room were all on the agenda, and the party seemed to have divided into three camps.

There were the sober, serious types, mostly talking shop and arguing about surgical techniques. They seemed to be in the sitting room, and from his position in the hall Adam began to wonder just how serious they were. They certainly weren't all that sober as the party wore on, and he hardly dared go in there.

Upstairs, the women had split up and taken some of the children each. The boys seemed to be in the boys' room, and the girls in Skye's. Anna was with Skye, and Allie was in there keeping her company and helping. Lissa and Sarah were in the boys' room, and they had by far the hardest job, Adam could tell.

He stuck his head round the door and winced. All the boys' things were piled in the middle of the room, and all round the sides the wallpaper was yielding to their endeavours—except that they were all short, and so the paper was only off on the bottom half.

'I thought you were good at this?' he said to Lissa with a grin.

'I am—I'm wonderful! Look behind the door.'

He looked, and found the wall clear. 'Fantastic!' he murmured. 'I'm amazed. So much order out of so much chaos!'

'Of course. Ben, stop that, please! Sorry, he's getting a bit hyper.'

'Maybe it's time for a break,' Adam suggested, mindful of the ordered-in pizza keeping hot in the oven. Afterwards, he was to wonder about his choice of words, but at the time it seemed logical.

'Right, everyone, downstairs,' Lissa ordered, and they whooped and skidded towards the door.

'Hey, steady, chaps,' Adam said, but he was ignored. Pizza was way up the list, long before listening to adults.

There was a crush, of course, and Ben and Danny got in a race. It probably would have been fine if Ben hadn't slipped on a bit of sticky paper on his shoe at the top of the stairs, but he did, and in horror they watched as he tumbled over and fell headlong. Then, suddenly, halfway down there was a cracking noise and he halted abruptly and screamed.

They all froze, and then Lissa's hands flew to her face and she started to shake. 'Oh, my God,' she whispered, and Adam pushed past her.

'It's OK, Ben,' he said, and went carefully down to the boy's level. Ben's arm was through the banisters and, needless to say, it was broken. He was sobbing now, and behind him Adam heard the sitting-room door open.

'What is it?'

'Ben—he's fallen downstairs and hurt his arm. He's all right, aren't you, sport? Let's get you out of here. Josh, can you give me a hand?'

'Sure. OK, little one, don't worry, Daddy's here.' He looked at Adam, his face ashen. 'What do you want me to do?'

'Just lift him up a little so I can get the arm through. He's broken the spindle—I can probably bend it out of the way. That might help.'

Seconds later the sobbing child was free, and Lissa was rushing down the stairs with tears in her eyes. 'Are you all right, darling? I'm here. Don't worry, it's all right.'

'It's a classic greenstick,' Adam said quietly. 'It'll need pulling out under anaesthetic and plastering, and I think he'll be fine. Can you feel all your fingers, Ben? Wiggle them for me.'

He wiggled them and nodded tearfully. 'It hurts.'

'I'm sure it does, Ben. I'm sorry. Well, you're going to have to go to hospital and be sorted out. Think you can cope with that?'

He nodded, and Adam looked up the stairs at Anna, who was holding Jasper by the hand. Damn Helle for leaving so suddenly, he thought. Still, she'd offered... 'Anna, I hate to do this to you, but could you watch them for me until I get back? Give everyone pizza and ice cream, and then—'

'Don't worry, we'll manage,' Anna said. 'You take Ben, and we'll sort out the rest.'

Well, they'd done it. They'd given everyone pizza, and then while the children ate ice cream and watched television in the breakfast room, the women organised a clear-up, gathering up bin bags of paper and mopping down floors, and the men moved the furniture back into position.

Matt and Sarah took their children home, and Allie and Mark left once they were sure everything was cleared up.

'Right, how about you three? Shall we see what your rooms look like?' Anna suggested.

'Messy,' Skye said heavily. 'I thought it would make it nice.'

'It will be nice,' Anna assured her. 'We've taken off most of the paper—a little bit longer and all the rest will be off, then you can have what you want on the walls. Have you decided?'

'No.'

A dismissal? Anna thought so, but it was hard to tell. Sometimes she wondered if Skye didn't dare express an opinion in case it was the wrong one. Was she so desperate for approval that she'd daren't hold a different view to anyone else?

Poor little mite, she thought.

'Still, at least the bed's made. Boys, what about your beds? Are they ready to get into?'

'Dunno.'

She followed them in and found their room similarly restored. Someone had been busy while she'd sat with the youngsters in the kitchen. She helped them change, wash and clean their teeth. Then she sent them to the loo and tucked them all up in bed.

Skye turned away when she went to kiss her, but Anna kissed her anyway, because she knew the child needed spontaneous displays of affection. 'Sleep tight, poppet,' she said, and turned her light down.

'Not too dark!' Skye said in alarm, and Anna turned it up again.

'OK?'

'Thanks. 'Night, Anna.'

'Goodnight, Skye. Sleep well—and well done. You've worked very hard today.'

She went downstairs, past the spot where poor little Ben Lancaster had caught his arm, and into the kitchen. It, too, was clear now, and there was nothing to do but sit and wait.

She went into the sitting room, bare and damp and smelling of wallpaper paste and soggy lime plaster, and dropped into the nearest chair. She was bushed, but even so she tried to stay awake for Adam coming home.

He might be hours. She knew that, and wondered if she wouldn't do better to go to bed, but she didn't want to—not in his house, with his children there. It wouldn't seem right. She moved to the sofa, pulled a throw off the back of it over herself and snuggled down with a cushion. She'd be fine like this until he got back...

Adam was exhausted. He'd been on the go all day, and just when he'd thought he was winding down he ended up in Theatre with little Ben Lancaster.

It was a straightforward enough break, and it didn't really take very long, but even so he'd been gone some three hours by the time he admitted defeat and plated it for a good result. It was trying to rotate, so he'd had little choice, but now he was wiped out and he just wanted to crawl into bed and sleep.

With Anna.

He let himself into his house, and found Anna in the sitting room under the throw. She should have gone up to bed, he thought, and then wondered where. In the au pair's room, without any bed linen? Or the spare room, where he'd slept last weekend when his parents had stayed?

Or his bed.

What a tempting thought.

Oh, lord, he thought, it's getting too cosy. She's here all the time—all day last Sunday, all day today, now tonight—it was getting too close, too much. The children were beginning to be a pain about her, especially Danny, and he didn't know what to do about it except keep her away.

He woke her with a kiss, like a princess in a fairytale, and, like a fairytale princess, she opened her eyes and looked at him and smiled.

'Hi. How is he?'

'Plated and in for a couple of days. It was a bit nasty. He'll be fine. I'm sorry to be so long.'

'It's all right. You look shattered. I'll get out of your hair now.' She stood up, picked up her coat and bag, which were by the door, and went up on tiptoe to kiss him goodnight.

'See you tomorrow,' she promised.

'I might get a babysitter.'

'Do that. Not your mother. Her eyes are too sharp.'

Adam chuckled, kissed her again, more thoroughly this time, and thanked her for looking after the party.

Then he watched her go, watched her walk out to her car and get in it and drive away, and wondered how he could be so perverse.

He'd wanted her to go, hadn't he? So why, then, was he so irrationally disappointed when she did?

# CHAPTER EIGHT

ANNA was on duty on the Sunday morning after Adam's party, and the first person she saw when she went in was Josh, sitting by Ben's bed and reading to him.

She went over to them and greeted them with a smile. 'Morning, all. How are things? How are you feeling, Ben?'

'It hurts,' he said fretfully.

Anna felt the tips of his fingers sticking out of the end of the cast. They were warm, not hot, and they wriggled when she touched them. Good.

His arm was in a special sling attached to the bed, the hand supported upright to minimise swelling, but it meant he couldn't fidget very easily and that was hard for a little boy, especially such an active one as Ben.

'He's all right,' Josh told her. 'He had a bit of a restless night. I stayed with him—Lissa's at home with Katie, stressing out. I've rung her a couple of times, but she doesn't believe he hasn't succumbed to the anaesthetic, I don't think.'

Anna smiled understandingly. 'Why don't you tell her to come in? She'll feel happier when she's seen him.'

'She's on her way. She wants to see the post-op X-rays—ah, here she is. Ben, Mummy's here.'

Anna turned to greet Lissa, and in the distance, just

coming onto the ward, she saw Adam with his three children in tow.

'It's a party,' she said with a smile, and waved at him.

The children waved back, all except Skye who looked around her worriedly and moved a step closer to Adam. Anna went over to them, leaving Lissa and Katie to talk to Ben and Josh in peace.

'Hi,' she said softly. 'Is this a social call, or are you working?'

'Bit of both. I thought I'd check up on him—how is he? I was a bit concerned about his circulation.'

'Seems good,' she told him. 'His fingers are nice and warm, and they're wriggling from time to time when he gets bored.'

'All the time, then, I should think, if Danny's anything to go by, eh, sport?'

'Is he going to be all right?' Skye asked, her eyes like saucers, studying the sling doubtfully.

'Yes,' Adam told her gently. 'He just needs time for the bones to join together again, then he'll have the little metal bits out that are holding them together at the moment, and he'll be as good as new.'

'Metal bits?' Danny asked, avidly interested.

Adam looked at Anna. 'Can we have the plates?'

'Sure.' She fetched the X-rays from the file trolley, and Adam snapped them into the light box on the wall near Ben's bed. 'Can you see, Ben? That's your arm, and here are the bones, and these white things are the little metal plates that hold the break together, and these little things are the screws. They'll come out in about four weeks, when you're better, and then you'll just have a cast on for the rest of the time.'

'Can I see the first ones again?' Josh asked, and Adam snapped the initial plates up onto the screen.

'Ow,' Lissa said under her breath, and Adam nodded.

'Ow, indeed. You can see why I had to operate—there's a distinct rotation here where he left his arm behind in the banisters and tried to keep on moving. In too much of a hurry for your pizza, weren't you, Ben? Never mind, I expect you can have some as soon as you get home.'

'Which will be when?' Josh asked.

Adam shrugged and pulled a thoughtful face. 'Couple of days? I'd like to get the swelling right down and get a proper cast on it, then he can get back to normal for a while.'

'He was lucky it wasn't a little further down towards his hand,' Josh said pensively, studying the plates. 'It would have hit the epiphysis and that would have been drastic.'

'What's the epiffy-thing?' Ben asked, looking from one to the other.

'The growth plate. There's a special place on each bone where it does its growing, and if you break it there it can stop growing properly. That doesn't matter when you're big, but when you're little it can be more of a problem,' Adam explained.

''Cos you'd end up with one short arm,' Danny said, his mind working visibly.

'That's right. There's a girl in here at the moment who did that to her leg, and it didn't grow, and now we're trying to make her leg grow longer with a special operation.'

'Did you do the operation?' Skye asked, speaking for the first time.

'Yes.'

'What's Jaz looking at?' Danny asked, and they looked round to see the little boy squatting under Damian, peering up through the cut-out in the Stryker bed at his face.

'That's Damian. He has to lie in a special bed at the moment. He gets very bored. I expect he'll be pleased to have someone to talk to. I take it the locks are all on it?'

'Oh, yes,' Anna assured him with a laugh. 'There's no way he can spin it round and dump Damian on the floor. Nevertheless, I think we might get him out from under it. Jaz, come here, sweetheart.'

He said goodbye to Damian, and came running over, throwing himself at Anna. She scooped him up into her arms with a laugh, swung him round and settled him on her hip, then looked up to see a steely expression on Adam's face.

'I'd better take these kids out of here,' he said tightly. 'Jasper, come on.'

Anna put him down and watched them as they left the ward, puzzled by their abrupt departure.

'Was it something I said?'

'God knows,' Josh murmured, moving to stand beside her. 'That man moves in mysterious ways. I think he panicked.'

'Panicked?'

'You're getting too close, Anna—hang in there. You're getting to him.'

'Oh, lord.' She tugged at her tabard, looked at her watch and straightened. 'Um, I have to go and get on. I've got to take report and get on with the day. I'll see you later.'

Too close, she thought, trying to ignore the hurt

Adam's abrupt departure had caused. How can I be too close? I love them, I love him, he loves me—how can we all *possibly* be too close?

Adam didn't come round that night, and she didn't see him until Monday afternoon, because she was on a late and he was in Theatre. He came round to do his post-op checks, though, looking harassed, and she confronted him.

'I thought you were coming round last night,' she said, trying not to sound accusing.

'I was—I'm sorry I didn't get to you, but Danny was sick and I didn't think it was fair to leave him with the babysitter.'

'You could have phoned.'

He nodded. 'I know. I'm sorry. I thought I'd finish stripping the sitting room and the night just got away from me. I didn't want to ring you at midnight.'

'I wouldn't have minded. I had a lie-in this morning.'

'Lucky you,' he said with a rueful smile. 'I didn't. The new nanny started today. I think she's going to be a disaster. I'd come round tonight but I need to be there. As if that wasn't bad enough, it's half-term week this week, and the kids are going to be at home all the time with her and I don't see it working.'

'Why don't I come to you?'

'No. I don't think that's a good idea. Not with the kids in the house. I might slide out if I can get away for a minute, but it will be a flying visit.'

Crumbs, Anna thought sadly. That's all he can spare—just the crumbs from his life.

He arrived at ten past ten, and his eyes showed the signs of his domestic strain.

'Problems?'

'Like you wouldn't believe,' he said, going into her arms with a sigh of relief. 'I'm sorry, this really is going to be a flying visit, but I just needed to see you, get a bit of sanity in my life.'

He eased away and tilted her chin, looking down into her eyes. He looks so unhappy and torn, Anna thought, and lifted a hand to caress his cheek. The stubble was rough against her palm, curiously erotic. She drew his head down for a kiss, and he took her mouth hungrily.

'How long can you stay?' she asked, and he laughed softly against her mouth.

'Long enough,' he murmured, and kissed her again.

He lied. It wasn't long enough. For ever wouldn't be long enough to give him all the love she had to give.

Ben made good progress, and went home on Tuesday morning, to his parents' relief. Lissa had found it very difficult to juggle Katie and Ben, and Josh had found it impossibly hard to see his patients and ignore Ben's pleas for attention every time he'd gone past his line of vision. They'd had to move Ben so that he hadn't been able to see his father so easily, and then Ben had got upset because Josh had been out of sight.

When Lissa took Ben home, Josh kissed him goodbye and watched them go with a sigh of relief.

'Thank God for that—now I can get on with my work without feeling guilty,' he said to Anna with a smile. He searched her face and the smile faded. 'How are things?'

She shrugged. 'Much the same. I don't know how long I can go on like this, Josh. I feel like a hamster in a cage, and he gets me out when he wants to play with me.'

'I think that's a bit harsh,' Josh said gently. 'He does have problems, Anna. Those kids need a lot of time and attention. Skye, especially, needs a lot of one-to-one.'

'She needs a mother,' Anna said tightly.

'She's had two already. Perhaps what she needs is just what Adam's giving her—stability and security. I hate to say it, but I wonder if I was wrong. I don't think it's right for Adam, but it might well be right for the children, and perhaps he's just about strong enough to do it—to make that sacrifice for the kids. In which case, Anna, you're going to get very badly hurt.'

'I know,' she said softly, her voice rough with tears. 'I don't agree about Skye, but I think you're right about Adam, and I think he's capable of hurting both of us if he feels it's what he has to do. Only time will tell.'

The phone rang, and she excused herself to answer it, then snapped into action. 'OK. Thank you. We'll start getting ready. We've got a few beds—not many. I'll see if I can mobilise a few discharges or cancel any operations. Thanks for letting me know.'

She looked up at Josh. 'A school bus has overturned. There are lots of orthopaedic injuries and some head injuries. They'll be coming in to A and E shortly. Can you clear any of your patients?'

He ran an eye over the ward. 'I don't know. You might want to contact Adam, see if he's got anyone that can go. I'll have a flick through the notes and think about it.'

She rang Adam in the outpatients clinic, and he

groaned. 'I've got a full clinic this morning—I'll have to leave them and go over to A and E to assess the kids as they come in. Damn. And that means I'll be home late, and the new nanny has to leave at six.'

'Do you want me to go round there?'

'No—I'll contact my mother. If I can't get hold of her, I might ask you. Thanks. As for the beds, I haven't got anyone I can transfer or discharge—unless we send Kate home. She's getting on all right with her leg and it's healed well. I was sending her home tomorrow, but she could go today. Go and talk to her mother, see what she says.'

'OK. I'll speak to you later.'

She found Allie, started her off on shuffling patients to get the spare beds all grouped together, and found Mrs Funnell and Kate. 'We've got a problem,' she told them. 'We need all the beds we can lay our hands on, and Mr Bradbury was going to suggest that Kate went home tomorrow. He thinks, in fact, she could go home today, if you feel you can cope and you're ready for it. Of course, you can always ring up or come in for advice. How do you feel?'

'I'd love to go home,' Kate confessed. 'I'm so bored in here. I want to go back to school.'

'Well, that might be a bit quick but you should be able to manage at home all right, I think. Do you need to ring anyone?'

'My car's here,' Mrs Funnell said. 'I can take her straight away.'

'Well, I think Mr Bradbury will come up and see you first—oh, here he is now.'

Their eyes met and they shared a brief but intimate smile. 'Kate's keen,' she said, and he grinned at the girl.

'How did I guess?' Adam looked at her leg, and nodded. 'You'll be fine,' he told her. 'Go home and enjoy yourself. Not too much weight-bearing, and you'll have to come back every day for physio, but you should be all right now. I'm sorry to hustle you, but I don't think you mind too much, do you?'

Kate grinned. 'Absolutely not. It's brilliant.'

He chuckled, winked at Anna as he turned away and then strode off, presumably to A and E. The phone rang again, and Anna left another nurse sorting out Kate's discharge notes and went to get the phone.

'Right,' she said, gathering them all together. 'First one's coming into A and E now. Make sure everything else that needs doing gets done. I'll deal with the new admissions. Allie, I want you to take over the running of the rest of the ward for now, please. Make sure nothing falls down the cracks. I don't want drugs forgotten and treatment neglected just because we're going to be rushed off our feet. And don't forget to smile at the children. They'll be scared, they'll be hurting. Their parents will be panic-stricken. Be calm and be kind, and keep your eyes open for anything that's been missed. Right, off you go.'

Adam went into A and E, looked around and found a cluster of doctors around Patrick Haddon, one of the A and E consultants. 'Right, we've got three orthopaedic teams on standby, including Adam Bradbury— Hello, Adam, come and join us. You know Robert Ryder, don't you, and his registrar David Patterson? You'll be the three teams. I want you to work together on the orthopaedic cases, prioritising and allocating them to your teams according to your areas of expertise. I know we've got one pelvic fracture coming in, and possibly others. There may be spinal injuries. Neuro are standing by for those, but I gather your Stryker bed is in use at the moment, Adam?'

'Yes, it is, but he's virtually ready to come off it. I could free it if it was absolutely necessary.'

'OK. We'll see. Lots of arms and legs, I expect. That's normal. There are internal injuries, of course—Nick, you're in charge of those. I want everyone triaged, stabilised, X-rayed and sorted as fast as possible—just don't miss anything in your hurry. Right, I can hear a siren—I think we're in business.'

It was chaotic, but they were so busy there wasn't time to notice. The pelvic fracture was nasty and needed external fixation, and Adam, scanning the plates of the other children who had been processed, decided he ought to take the pelvis. He was just about to pull the plates off the light box when he noticed a tiny, almost invisible little line across one of the vertebrae.

'I want another view of this,' he said to the radiographer. 'Very, very carefully. It looks like a very unstable fracture. Don't shuffle him about.'

'OK. What view do you want?'

'Lateral, please—and oblique. Might pick up more.'

He was right. It was a fracture through the vertebral body of the fourth lumbar vertebra, and the lateral view showed a segment of bone poised to slice into the spinal cord.

'That will need fixing,' he said to Robert Ryder. 'I want a CT scan before I do anything, and he needs to stay on the spinal board. He'll need blood crossmatched. Those pelvic fractures will be bleeding heavily into the tissues.'

'You'll have to fight the neuros for the scanner. They've got a couple of head injuries.'

'We can wait for them. I need to do a couple of others first, I think. He's not that urgent, he's just critical. What else have we got?'

They scanned through the notes, went round and saw the injuries at first hand and then they started in earnest.

Adam's first case was a nasty fracture of the hand and arm, and he worked for two hours to restore the circulation and realign the bones to his satisfaction. That case was followed by his pelvic and spinal fracture patient. After studying the CT scan, he decided how to tackle the vertebral body and went in carefully through the abdomen, meaning to tackle the bone from in front of the cord.

'Pressure's crashing,' the anaesthetist warned. 'Have you got a bleed there?'

'I reckon. Whoops,' he said as they opened the abdomen. 'I think we have a major leak. Can we have four units in here fast, please? This kid's going to bleed to death. Where the hell is it coming from? Can I have some more suction? Thank you.'

It was a race against time, but finally he found the leak, a vessel that had been ruptured by the end of one of the pelvic bones. Once it was stopped, they could begin to work on the patient again, and Adam focused on him and forgot about everything else.

There was no time to worry about the patients that were waiting, or the nanny his children hated, or whether his mother would get the answerphone message.

* * *

Anna stayed on after the end of her shift, checking head injury cases every few minutes for change in status, monitoring possible internal injuries, providing post-op care to the minor orthopaedic cases that came back from Theatre.

She gathered that there was a boy with a spinal fracture that Adam was fixing, who also had a severely broken pelvis. She wondered how on earth they were going to nurse him, and then Adam appeared, rubbing his eyes and flexing his shoulders.

'You look bushed.'

'I am bushed—what are you still doing here?'

'Helping out. They're rushed off their feet, I could hardly go. Have you spoken to your mother yet?'

'No—I'm going to do that now. I'll ring home and see if there's been blood-letting. What have you got for me, or are they still down in A and E?'

'Two fractures—an arm and a leg. Displaced fracture of the olecranon, and a femur. Simple fracture.'

'Brilliant,' he said, rolling his eyes. 'I hate elbows. OK. I'll do the femur first. Keep the elbow still and give pain relief—is it written up?'

'I believe so. She's crying.'

'I'm sure she is. If I'd yanked off the end of my funny bone, I reckon I'd be crying.'

He disappeared into the office and came out a minute later looking ragged. 'My mother's there. The nanny's gone. She's sacked her. She smacked Jasper this morning because he was crying. Mum's reported her to the agency. What the hell do I do now?'

'Your femur and your elbow. Your mother is quite capable. Don't worry.'

'And what about tomorrow?'

'Bring them in. They can sit here and watch telly

and do drawings and play with the others. It won't be a problem. Go and operate.'

Adam flashed her a weary smile and headed off towards the corridor. Anna carried on with her post-op and pre-op care, checking drips, calming parents, and it was hours before the ward settled to something approaching normality.

She went home, ate a sandwich in the bath and crawled into bed. She was just dropping off to sleep when the phone rang, and she stretched out an arm and grabbed the receiver.

'Hello?'

'Hi.'

Her heart did its usual jig, and a smile curved her lips. She settled down with a contented sigh. 'Hi. How was it all in the end? Done your elbow to your satisfaction?'

'Yup. Done it all. I'm home, finally.'

'How are the kids?'

'Asleep. I'm going to ring the agency in the morning and give them hell. I've bribed my parents to stay until the weekend, but they go to Florida on Tuesday. That gives me not quite a week to sort something out.' He sighed. 'Do you know, I can quite see why women don't make it up the career ladder. It would be so much easier if I were self-employed or had a less pressured job.'

She could have told him the answer, but he didn't want to hear it, and she was sick of throwing herself against that particular brick wall. 'Have a bath and go to bed,' she told him.

'I'm in the bath,' Adam said. 'With the cordless phone and a glass of wine. Bliss.'

'I'm in bed,' she said softly.

She heard his indrawn breath, and smiled.

'Did I wake you?'

'Not really. I don't mind, anyway. It's nice to talk to you.'

'I wish I was there with you,' he said softly. 'I could do with a hug.'

'Only a hug?' she asked, and he gave a low chuckle.

'OK. I confess.'

'I wish you were here, too,' she admitted. 'I never used to mind sleeping alone.'

'Close your eyes and pretend I'm there.' Her lids drifted shut, powerless to resist, and he carried on talking, driving her crazy with his soft, hypnotic voice. 'Imagine I'm touching you, running my hands over you, feeling your skin burn against my palms. Imagine my body—'

'Adam?'

There was a startled grunt, followed by a splash and a muttered curse.

Anna's eyes flew open, and she started to laugh. 'Is that your mother?'

'Yes—I'm on the phone,' he said through the door.

'Oh. Right. I've made tea.'

'Thanks.'

She heard the footsteps retreating, and the sound of his muffled laughter. 'I could kill her. I nearly dropped the phone in the bath.'

'She's lovely.'

'She's everywhere.' He sighed, and lowered his voice. 'I want you.'

She swallowed. 'I know. Why don't you sneak out? Tell her you need to buy milk or something, or you need a walk.'

'I could tell her I need to come and see you. She'd love it. She hasn't stopped talking about you since the day after the ball.'

'So why don't you?' she asked softly, but she knew he wouldn't.

He gave a quiet sigh, and for a moment he was silent. When he spoke, she could tell he was back to reality, back to his responsibilities and duties. 'No. I'll see you tomorrow. Are you on early?'

'No, I'm on a late.'

'Fancy a wake-up call?'

'Adam!'

'What? Oh, damn. Yes, Mum, I'm coming!' He sighed again and gave a lazy, sexy chuckle. 'I wish. I'll see you tomorrow. Sleep tight.'

'What on earth?'

Anna slid her legs over the side of the bed, grabbed her dressing-gown and ran downstairs, shoving her hair out of her eyes with one hand as she fumbled for the door.

'Breakfast,' Adam said, pushing the door shut and pulling her into his arms.

She laughed and looked up at him through bleary eyes. 'You're crazy. I was asleep—it's only half past six!'

'I'm sorry.' He cupped her chin, his thumb absently caressing her cheek. 'I missed you last night. That phone conversation did nothing for my sleep patterns.'

'I'm sure. I had some pretty colourful dreams myself.' She ran her tongue over her teeth and pulled a face. 'I need five minutes in the bathroom. Put the kettle on, there's a love.'

She ran upstairs, showered rapidly and cleaned her teeth, then came out to find Adam naked in her bed with a tray of fresh, steaming tea and a plate of chocolate-filled croissants on his lap.

He patted the mattress beside him. 'Breakfast in bed,' he said with a slow smile, and her heart thumped.

'Sounds good.'

'It will be,' he promised, and moved the tray out of the way. 'You can eat later. That's dessert.'

Anna had a silly smile on her face all day. Adam had only been there an hour, but it had been the most wonderful hour of her life to date. The memory carried her through a difficult shift, with every bed full and many of their little patients in quite critical condition.

The boy with the fractured spine and pelvis was being nursed flat in a bed with a special mattress, because he couldn't be turned due to the external fixator on his pelvis. He was catheterised because of bruising to his bladder nerves, and his legs were tingly and funny, he said, but all in all he'd escaped lightly.

Adam had been to see them all and was satisfied with their progress. He was wonderful with the parents, Anna thought, watching him in action. He explained just enough, so that they didn't feel patronised and yet understood what he'd had to do and why.

It was a skill a lot of doctors didn't have, Anna knew, but it didn't surprise her that Adam had it. He seemed to have a natural ability to communicate, and a real empathy for the parents.

Little Emily Parker with her brittle bone disease

was the only one he was really concerned about, and yet she was making progress. It was just slower than he'd hoped, and he was concerned about her chest.

'It's very compromised,' he murmured. 'Those ribs are a very funny shape. There's no way she can be getting any real movement through them, so all her breathing's abdominal.'

'The prognosis is pretty awful, isn't it?' Anna said thoughtfully.

'I would say she's on a knife edge,' Adam admitted. 'I don't know what will get her in the end—a cough, probably. She'll end up with fluid on her lungs and drown. Just keep her away from anyone with a cold.'

It wasn't possible. On Thursday she started coughing, and on Friday morning, when Anna went in, her bed was empty.

'Where's Emily gone?' she asked the night sister, a dreadful suspicion forming in her mind.

'Ah. We lost her at three o'clock this morning. She got pneumonia. Her lungs filled, and then she arrested. Adam tried to resuscitate her but he couldn't get her back. He was gutted.'

Anna sat down with a bump. 'Oh, damn,' she said heavily. She thought of the gutsy little girl with her terribly deformed bones, and her dedicated mother who had spent most of the past six years protecting the fragile child from the world. And now she was gone, wiped out, taken by some trivial and inconsequential cold.

'It was inevitable,' the night sister said pragmatically. 'It was bound to happen, Anna.'

'I know,' she said, but that didn't stop it getting to her. After she'd taken report, she went into the kitchen, howled, blew her nose, washed her face and got out her rescue kit. That was where Adam found her, dabbing concealer under her eyes. She looked at him in the mirror then put it down and turned and took him in her arms.

'I'm sorry, love,' Anna said tenderly, and he hugged her hard. She could feel the tension in him, feel the pain still looking for a way out.

'Come and see me tonight,' she said, and he nodded.

'I will.' He moved out of her arms and slumped against the edge of the worktop with a harsh sigh. 'How many patients have I lost? How many times have I gone through this process? You'd think I'd get used to it.'

'I'm glad you haven't. I think it makes you a better doctor.'

Adam gave her a crooked smile. 'I don't know about that, but I think it makes me a better parent. I went home and stood in Skye's room and looked at her, and wondered how I'd feel if it had been her. They were the same sort of age—Emily was a little older, although you would never have known that from looking at her.'

He looked down at his hands, hands that had failed, and sighed again. 'I know it had to happen, I know it was a blessing in disguise, I know she'd suffered terribly in her life and was lucky to have survived so long. It still hurts.'

'I know. Want to borrow my lipstick? It works for me.'

He laughed softly and hugged her again. 'You're a treasure. I'll see you tonight, if not before. I might even come clean with my mother and spend the evening with you. How would that be?'

'Lovely,' she said, and wondered what it was really like to be a hamster in a cage and be taken out occasionally for the odd run around before being put back again.

She stopped her train of thought there. Adam was stressed enough, torn in all directions, and it wouldn't help at all if she was sulking because he couldn't tear himself into even more bits. He needed her. That was all that mattered at the moment.

He needed her, and she loved him. There was nothing more to say.

## CHAPTER NINE

ADAM took Anna to a quiet country pub, where they sat in the corner by a log fire, and he dropped his head back against the wall and sighed. He was tired—tired, and sad, and worried about the children.

'What a day,' he mumbled.

'How are the kids?' she asked, zooming in on his main concern with her usual accuracy.

He shut his eyes and groaned. 'Don't. I still don't have a nanny sorted out. I rang the agency and told them what I thought of them, so that takes care of them as a source of child care.'

'Oops. Bit firm, were you?'

He met her eyes and dredged up a laugh. 'Just a bit. Put it like this, I don't think they're in any doubt about my feelings. Then I tried the au pair agency again and they've promised me someone, but they can't do anything for at least a fortnight, and my parents are going to Florida in three days' time.'

He picked up his beermat and shredded it absently. 'What do I do, Anna?' he asked with studied calm. 'Do I give up work?'

'Don't be silly!' she exclaimed. 'You can't—you're too valuable. What would your patients do without you? Your gifts are too great to be wasted, Adam. You have to work.'

Strange, how her words warmed him and made him feel better. Some things, though, couldn't be made better. 'I lost Emily,' he said.

'You didn't lose her, Adam,' she pointed out gently. 'She was already lost when she was born. Taking responsibility for that is assuming too much. You simply aren't that omnipotent. Leave that sort of thing with God, where it belongs.'

'I could be a carpenter,' he suggested, and Anna had a feeling he was only half joking.

'I doubt if you're good enough. Wood doesn't heal.'

He suppressed a smile. 'Are you insinuating that my carpentry skills aren't up to scratch?' he said indignantly. 'Damn cheek.'

'I'm sure they're wonderful. It doesn't help your problem, though. You need a solution in three days,' she reminded him, 'and carpentry isn't it.'

Adam sighed and rammed a hand through his hair, leaving it rumpled. 'So what do you suggest?' he asked. 'The hospital crèche is too crowded to take them and, anyway, they need to get to and from school. Besides, that doesn't solve the problem of what I do at night when I'm on call. I need live-in help. I can't get the kids up in the middle of the night and bring them with me every time.'

'I could stay with you,' she suggested.

He was tempted—very tempted—but not because it solved anything. 'How does that help?' he asked sceptically. 'You go to work as well.'

'And they're at school. I work from seven to three by choice. That means if they come to work with you at eight or thereabouts, they could get a taxi to school from the hospital, and I could pick them up at the end of the day. You could get home whenever you get home, I'll be there at night when you're on call, and there'd be the added bonus that we'd see each other every evening.'

They would indeed. He looked at her thoughtfully. 'You really mean it, don't you?' he said in quiet amazement. 'You'd do it.'

She rolled her eyes. 'Well, of course I mean it! Why would I not?'

Adam searched her eyes for an age, then looked away, shaking his head. He could get addicted to her presence, and so could the kids. 'No. It's not a good idea.'

'Have you got a better one?'

'No,' he told her honestly. 'No, I haven't.' He thought of the children growing dependent on her, and asked himself how much difference two short weeks could make. Surely they wouldn't get addicted that fast? 'It's only very temporary, I suppose,' he said thoughtfully. 'Just until the new au pair comes in a fortnight.'

'Was that a yes?' Anna asked.

He shrugged. 'I don't see I've got a choice,' he said heavily. He knew he wasn't being very gracious, but the thought of Anna there all the time was so tempting he thought it was clouding his judgement, and he was busy looking for the pitfalls. 'It's not ideal, but it solves nearly every problem. Can you switch your rota for the next two weeks so you're on earlies?'

She laughed softly. 'I can do what I like with the darned rota. It's my responsibility. I devise it. Certainly I can change it.'

'I might have to take you up on your offer, then,' he said with a smile, and she held out her hand.

'Done,' she said, as he shook it, and he felt a huge burden lifting off his shoulders.

Whatever the drawbacks, however foolish it might be, at least he would know his children were safe, and that had to be the most important thing.

He lifted her hand to his lips and kissed her palm. 'You're a wonderful woman, do you know that?' he said quietly, and soft colour brushed her cheeks.

'I just want to be able to get my hands on you day and night,' Anna said, laughing dismissively, and he thought of the nights, when the children were asleep, and the hot rush of desire nearly choked him.

Adam swallowed hard and picked up his glass, draining it. 'Another one?' he asked. 'Or do you want to wait and have wine with our meal?'

'You're driving.'

'I'm always driving. I don't need to drink. What about you?'

'Neither do I. Spring water would be fine, thanks.'

She handed him her glass and smiled up at him, and he wondered how he was going to survive having her at home.

No. That would be easy. The hard bit would be letting her go, and it suddenly dawned on him that he might have made a dreadful mistake.

Anna moved in on Sunday evening, to the children's great delight and excitement. She brought with her only the clothes that she'd need and the food left in the fridge, because her house was only a mile or so away and she could pop back for anything else, so 'moving in' was a bit of an exaggeration, but the children thought it was great fun.

They helped carry her case and bag up to the attic,

and Skye put her wash things out in the shower room while Jasper passed her the underwear from her little bag and Danny struggled to put her blouses on hangers.

She gave him a hand once the underwear had been put away in the chest of drawers, and then there was a knock on the door and Adam appeared with a tray of tea, juice and biscuits. The children swooped on them instantly.

'I thought refreshments might be in order, but you'll need to be quick,' he said, and she met his eyes over the children's heads and smiled.

'Thanks. Forget the biscuits, but I'm gasping for a cup of tea.' He handed her a mug and she cupped her hands round it, sipping gratefully. 'Mmm. Wonderful. Just what I needed.' She looked around her and sighed softly. 'This is a lovely room. I'm going to like staying here,' she said in contentment.

'Have you got everything you need?'

Everything, she thought. Him, the children…

'I'm sure I have. If not I can ask, can't I, kids? You'll help me.'

'You've got loo paper and soap—I checked,' Skye told her soberly.

'Thank you, darling. That's kind.'

'I helped Daddy make the bed,' Danny said proudly. 'He gave you his quilt cover!'

Adam laughed a little awkwardly. 'It's the only one without rips, I think. Our washing line at the other house was a bit near the fence, and there was a nail sticking out of it that used to catch the clothes. I keep meaning to go shopping, but I suppose I might as well wait and get something that goes with whatever we do to the rooms.'

'That makes sense.'

Anna smoothed her hand lightly over the fabric. His quilt cover. That would destroy any chance she might have had to sleep! 'It's very kind of you to be so considerate,' she said, rather touched that all of them seemed to have gone to so much trouble over her visit.

'I polished the table,' Jasper said in satisfaction. 'See.'

She did. She saw shiny places, and places with dust on, and little fingerprints all over most of it. 'It's lovely,' she said with a lump in her throat. 'Thank you, Jaz. Thank you, all of you.'

'Right, you lot, downstairs and get ready for bed. I'll come down and see you in a minute.'

They trailed off, grumbling gently, and Adam pushed the door to and sat down sideways on the bed next to her, one knee hitched up. 'Are you sure you've got all you need?' he asked again, and she nodded.

'Sure. Do you want me to get the children ready for bed now?'

He looked faintly startled. 'Good grief, no!'

'No? So what do you want me for?' she asked curiously, and he gave a strangled laugh.

'Apart from the obvious?'

Warm colour slid up her throat and touched her cheeks, and he leant forward and brushed her lips with his.

'Apart from the obvious,' she echoed, her heart pattering in her chest.

He shrugged. 'Just the end of the day, like we said. If you just pick them up from school and bring them home and make sure they're safe, that's all I need. I don't expect you to do anything except act as a safety net. You might want to cook the odd meal, but even that I'm not bothered about.'

Adam reached out a hand and cupped her cheek, and she turned her face into his hand and kissed it lingeringly.

'It's good to have you here,' he said gruffly. 'Thank you, Anna. It's a huge weight off my mind. The children's safety and happiness are so important to me—I feel so responsible for them.'

'I know you do. Does anyone ever tell you what a good father you are to your children?'

He looked away, a wry and slightly self-conscious smile quirking his lips. 'Not often, but it's not why I do it, so I don't need the accolades. I just do my best. Sometimes it's not enough, but most of the time we get by.'

'They're lucky to have you.'

His mouth tightened. 'Not as lucky as they thought they were going to be. It's difficult sometimes, being alone, but it beats being held to ransom.'

He stood up and retrieved the tray from the floor, gathered up the mugs and glasses and headed for the door. 'I'll see you later. Come on down when you're ready for some company.'

It was odd, Anna thought, watching the empty doorway. She didn't know where she stood with him while she was in this role. Normally she would have gone downstairs and made herself at home with him, but tonight she felt a little shy and awkward, as if she should be staying in her room like the hired help.

It was absurd. She knew it was absurd, and yet she felt as if she didn't belong, and she realised why Helle had been homesick. It would be so easy to feel you had to stay up here out of his way.

'Anna, what time do you want to eat?'

She went out onto the landing and hung over the banisters. Adam was standing at the top of the first flight of stairs, looking up at her, and she felt suddenly silly for her reticence. Of course he expected her to join him!

'Whenever,' she said. 'Do you want me to cook it?'

He shook his head. 'I was going to get a take-away. I've fed the children—I thought we could have a Chinese or Indian.'

'Sounds good.'

Blow the unpacking, she thought. A few pairs of trousers and jeans weren't going to come to any harm. She ran downstairs in her socks and joined him in the kitchen.

'Have a look at the menu,' he said, and they haggled over what they wanted and then later stole each other's choices anyway. And then it was time for bed and suddenly she really *didn't* know what he expected of her.

With the children in the house, she felt it would hardly be appropriate as their relationship stood for her to sleep openly with him. On the other hand, she wasn't sure if sneaking around and being deceitful was actually any better.

'I'll see you to your door,' he said in an undertone as she paused at the bottom of the attic stairs. His mouth tipped in a sexy smile. 'It's only courteous.'

'Of course,' she agreed with an answering smile, and tiptoed up so as to not disturb the children.

Once up there, he ushered her into her room, closed

the door and leant back against it, drawing her into his arms.

'I've been wanting to kiss you for hours,' he confessed, and, threading his hands through her hair, he scattered kisses over her brow and lids and cheekbones, over the plane of her jaw, down over the sensitive skin of her throat.

'Adam,' she whispered urgently, and he lifted his head and found her mouth, answering her plea. Her hands settled on his chest, feeling the solid warmth of his body so near—

'Daddy?'

He dragged his mouth from hers, his breathing ragged. 'Yes, darling,' he called through the door. 'I'm upstairs. I'm coming down now.' He kissed Anna again, just briefly, and gave a rueful wink. 'Sleep well, sweetheart. I'll see you in the morning.'

He went out, closing the door softly behind him, and she went to bed alone but happy. Adam was near, very near, and he seemed to be mellowing.

For the first time since he'd told her they were going nowhere, she felt a glimmer of hope. Cherishing it, she fell asleep and didn't wake until he called her in the morning.

That Monday Adam took Damian back down to Theatre and completed the surgery to his spine that would hold it in the final position, and then he removed the halo from his skull and the lower half of the frame from his pelvis.

Damian was now as straight as he could be made, and he needed mobilisation and physiotherapy to get him back onto his feet. Adam wondered how much taller he would be. Typically, it was a couple of centimetres, but Damian had been more distorted than most and the gain might be more.

Whatever, he was sure the boy would appreciate having his mobility restored and being shot of the restrictive Stryker bed and halo traction. He'd be able to turn his head, and look around, and sit, and walk with help—a great change from the immobility of the last three weeks.

His bed was next to that of Richard Lewis, the boy with the fractured pelvis and spine, who had regained sensation rapidly following the accident and would make a complete recovery.

In the meantime, Richard had to lie still, and Damian could spend some time with him and entertain him. Adam was sure Anna would find a way of bringing them together usefully.

She was wonderful with the kids, Adam thought. She managed them all so well—the sick, the crotchety, the bored. She kept them cheerful, yet disciplined and under control. She was a natural with them, and with his own, and he thought again that she would be the most wonderful mother.

The thought brought a pain he'd thought he'd forgotten, with an intensity he didn't remember.

He wanted to see her swollen with his child.

It took his breath away, the pain. He dragged in some air, and tipped his head back, rolling his shoulders and flexing them.

'You all right, Adam?' the anaesthetist asked.

'Yes—just a bit stiff. I need to move around for a minute. Perhaps you could close?' he said to his registrar, and, stripping off his gloves, he left the operating room and went out into the corridor, resting his head back against the cool wall and closing his eyes.

Damn. He'd thought he was over it, thought he'd come to terms with it, and in many ways he had, but there was something basic and primitive in him that needed to pass on his genes. He understood, he could rationalise it to death, but it didn't make it any easier.

He wanted to give Anna a child, and he couldn't.

And because he couldn't, she'd leave him. Maybe not now, maybe not for years, but she was only twenty-eight. What about when she was thirty-eight? When the sands of time had run away for another ten years, what then? Would she feel the pressure of that last trickle of sand in the egg-timer?

When had she become so important to him? When had he allowed her so close that she'd sneaked up inside him and become a part of him?

Two weeks, he told himself. In two weeks the new au pair would come, and Anna would move out. And then, Adam told himself, he'd stop seeing her. Stop going round to her house and making love to her in her beautiful candle-lit bedroom, stop flirting with her and teasing her and kissing her every chance he got.

It was unfair to her to trap her, to use her, to keep her on a string for his own benefit, no matter how much he needed her. He had to sever the link, cut her off, let her go for her own sake. He had to be cruel to be kind.

He swallowed the lump in his throat, and shrugged away from the wall. His registrar wasn't good enough to sew up Damian's incision. It had been reopened, and it was harder to make a neat job under those circumstances. He owed it to Damian to do the best job he could.

He scrubbed again, donned new gown and gloves and went back into the operating room.

* * *

Adam was busy that week with emergencies, and so Anna hardly saw Adam on the ward. Damian was mobile at last, and loving every minute of it, and although he was still in a certain amount of pain, the freedom more than made up for it.

Richard, the boy with the spinal and pelvic injuries, was the same age, and they struck up a friendship which Anna encouraged. Adam, on one of his flying visits to the ward, remarked on it to her.

'It's good for Damian, too,' Anna said thoughtfully. 'He was entertained by the others when he was trapped, and I think he realises it's a chance to give back some of what was given to him. Hopefully he won't get bored before Richard's a bit more mobile.'

'Mmm. I want to keep him pretty still for a while longer. That spinal fracture was pretty unstable and I know I've wired it together, but it may not be adequate if he does too much too soon. It does need time to heal. We'll give him another week and then I'll get it scanned again and see how much it's healed. That's one thing about kids—they do heal incredibly fast.'

'How's Ben Lancaster, by the way?' she asked. 'Have you seen him again?'

'Yes, Lissa brought him in yesterday to have the stitches out and a new cast. It's looking good. He'll have the plates out in another couple of weeks and he'll be fine. I'm pleased. The arm's nice and straight, which is a miracle when you think how bent and twisted it was when he fell. I must mend that banister, by the way. Remind me to glue it tonight.'

'Write it on your hand,' she suggested with a smile, and he laughed.

'That'll look good in my clinic! I'll just rely on

your wonderful memory,' he said, and then checked his watch and sighed. 'I have to go, talking of clinics. I've had a couple of patients added onto the beginning of the list that I thought I should see urgently. One's a knee following a ski injury. The GP's written "IDK" on the letter. I'm not sure if that means "internal destruction of the knee" or "I don't know"—could be either!

'The other's a baby with bilateral CDH. I may have to operate on her hips pretty soon, if the letter from her new GP is anything to go by. Apparently, it's been missed until now, and speed is of the essence with these congenital dislocations.'

'Will you do both cases tomorrow?' Anna asked, and he shrugged.

'I don't know. How are we for beds? Most of the school bus kids havc gonc—havc wc got any capacity? I've got three others booked already.'

She ran a mental eye over the ward, thinking of the tonsils, grommets and appendectomies that would be going home. 'A little. An extra two would fit, if we don't have a rash of emergencies. It might change by tomorrow, of course.'

'I'll check. I'll book them provisionally if I think they need it. The ski knee will be quick, I suspect, probably an arthroscopy. The baby might take longer. I'll keep you posted.'

After Adam had gone she checked the list of patients again to make sure she'd got beds available, and when he rang from the clinic at ten to three she confirmed that, emergencies permitting, they would have room for his extra two cases.

'Good. I've told them I'll ring them in the morning if I can't do it. They're coming in at eight, starved and ready to prep—I thought that was better than having them overnight unnecessarily, just in case we need the beds for something else. Are you going home now?'

'Shortly. Don't worry, I haven't forgotten the children.'

She heard his low chuckle. 'Sorry. It's hard to stop worrying. Old habits die hard.'

'Like old soldiers. Relax, Adam, it's all under control. We'll see you later.'

Anna hung up the phone, handed over the keys to Allie and left. As she drove to Jasper's nursery school, she found herself humming softly. It was just what she needed. Previously, when she'd gone off duty, the rest of the day had seemed to hang on her hands sometimes.

Now it was full, and not only full but fulfilling. She realised she was having a ball. The children were wonderful, and she was having more fun with them than she could have imagined. The boys were warm and spontaneous and cuddly, and even Skye was starting to mellow.

Life was better than it had been for years. Possibly better than ever.

'Anna, could you help me do my bedroom?' Skye asked on Wednesday after school, when Adam was still at work.

'Of course. What do you want to do?'

'Finish the walls—the paper's all half-off and I want to make it tidy and nice. Daddy's done the sitting room—it's all ready now for the wallpaper, he says, but it looks much better. I know we can't stick on the paper, but can we make it clean like that?'

'Of course,' Anna agreed, and they spent the next couple of evenings scraping damp wallpaper while the boys played around underfoot and shot each other with mock guns made of cardboard tubes.

And by Friday night, it was filled and sanded and ready for painting or papering.

'I want it all pretty cream and pink,' Skye told her. 'Daddy says it can be painted, but I want it all swirly.'

'We can do swirly with paint,' Anna said confidently, and demonstrated some ragging and sponging techniques for Skye.

'Like that,' Skye said about the colourwashing. 'In pink and cream.'

And so on Saturday afternoon, when Adam came home from the hospital, Anna was up a ladder with Skye below her on the lower part of the wall, and they were painting.

'Good grief,' he said faintly, hesitating, dumbstruck, in the doorway.

'Hi,' Anna said, brushing a strand of paint-streaked hair out of her eyes. 'I hope you don't mind—Skye asked if I could give her a hand, so we're having a go at colourwashing.'

'So I can see,' he said, bemused. 'Um, want a hand? I'll change.'

'Thanks.'

He was back in a minute or two, dressed in scruffy jeans with a rip in the knee and dribbles of paint all over them, and Anna realised he was no stranger to decorating. 'I'll start the woodwork,' he said, and, picking up a piece of discarded sandpaper, he moved in on the window.

It took the whole weekend, but by Sunday night Skye was back in her bedroom and it looked lovely.

'All you need now is a new carpet and some curtains,' Adam told her. 'You'll have to choose them next weekend—and then, I suppose, we should tackle the boys' room.'

'We', Anna thought, and wondered if that included her. She thought so, and felt warm inside.

'What about your room?' she asked as they went downstairs when the children were settled. 'Are you going to do anything with that?'

'Not yet,' he said with a weary laugh. 'Not until the sitting room and kitchen and hallway are sorted out, and the boys' room is finished, and I've refitted both bathrooms.'

'Not this week, then,' she said with a smile, and he laughed again, hugging her to his side.

'No, not this week. Thanks for helping Skye. You're a star.'

'My pleasure.'

He pushed the kitchen door shut, turned her into his arms and kissed her hungrily. 'I miss you,' he said gruffly after a long, lingering moment, resting his forehead against hers. 'We never seem to get any private time any more.'

'We could go to my house—we could ask one of the girls next door to babysit,' she suggested.

His eyes darkened, and he kissed her again. 'You're full of good ideas,' he murmured, and then they heard Skye's footsteps overhead and he straightened and moved away from her, going to the bottom of the stairs and looking up. 'Are you all right, Skye?'

Her voice drifted down from upstairs. 'Just going to the loo,' she said, and he came back and sighed.

'I'll get a babysitter,' he said with a chuckle. 'This is trashing my nerves.'

Of course, if they weren't trying to pretend that there was nothing between them, Anna thought later, there wouldn't be a problem. If the children came into the room and found them in each other's arms, it wouldn't matter. It wouldn't matter if they were married—it would be expected.

She looked at the shower cubicle in her own bathroom, and sighed. She wanted a bath. She just fancied lying down and having a long, hot soak.

Surely Adam wouldn't mind? She changed into her dressing-gown and went downstairs, washbag and towel in hand. He was just coming out of Skye's bedroom, and she asked if it was all right.

'Of course it's all right. I was just thinking the same thing. You go first, I'll follow you. I'll have your water—the tank's not that efficient and the kids have already had a bath. Give me a knock when you've finished.'

Anna nodded and went into the bathroom, filled the bath with steaming water and soaked for as long as she felt was fair. It felt wonderful, but Adam was waiting, and after all it was his bath. She washed quickly, dried herself, wound her hair into a turban and went along to his room, tapping softly on the door.

He opened it instantly and came out, a tender smile on his face. 'You're all wet,' he murmured, and brushed a little trickle away from her throat with his thumb. It dragged slightly against her skin, astonishingly erotic, and he bent his head and took her mouth in a searing, mind-blowing kiss that left her shaken to her foundations.

'Dear God, I want you,' he said unsteadily, and his eyes seemed to scorch her already heated skin. They tracked to the neck of her dressing-gown, which had fallen open to reveal the soft swell of her breasts, and his lids grew heavy with desire. 'I'll come to you later,' he promised in a charged undertone. 'After midnight, when the children are really asleep.'

'OK.' She backed away, her eyes locked with his, then turned and ran lightly up the stairs to her room, need pouring through her. The waiting was agonising. It was hours before she heard his footsteps on her landing, and then he slid into bed beside her, his body hot and taut and needy.

There were no preliminaries. They weren't necessary. She reached for him and took him in her arms, and he moved over her and entered her with one swift, desperate thrust. She wrapped her arms around him tighter, clinging to him as he drove them both over the brink.

'I love you,' he said rawly, as if the words were torn from him without permission, and then his body shuddered against hers, and his arms tightened convulsively as if he were trying to hold her close against him for ever.

The tears she'd held in check spilled over, and she laid a tender, fervent kiss against his stubbled cheek. 'I love you,' she whispered, and his mouth found hers in a kiss that seemed full of desperation.

He said her name almost soundlessly, reverently, and then, with one last, lingering kiss, he left her.

Anna lay without moving, her emotions raw. What had happened? Something was different, some element of desperation and despair. A terrible foreboding filled her, a deep fear that something had changed or was about to change, and that she was going to lose Adam.

You're getting paranoid, she told herself crossly. Nothing's changed.

And yet, if that was so, why had their emotions been so intense—and why, when he'd said her name, had it sounded like a prayer?

## CHAPTER TEN

ANNA wasn't wrong. Something *had* changed. After that night Adam didn't come to her again, neither did he take up her suggestion that they should get a babysitter and take some time out at her house.

In itself that didn't matter. She didn't miss their love-making so much as the closeness it brought, and that was missing in other parts of their lives as well.

Gone were the fleeting touches, the stolen kisses in the pantry, the little pats on the bottom as she passed him on the landing. Instead, she caught the occasional brooding look, and sometimes she surprised a look of sadness in his eyes.

He's going to end it, she thought. He's just waiting until the new au pair comes, and he's going to end it.

She felt sick at the thought, and so she buried herself in her work, helped the children with their homework, started on the decorating in the boys' room and fell into bed exhausted each night.

Adam was out later and later, going back to the hospital at every opportunity, and even Danny noticed it.

'Why is Daddy so busy?' he asked on Thursday evening. He was pushing pasta shapes around his plate, and Anna looked at him closely.

Poor little love, she thought. They're all so fragile, so emotionally vulnerable. Every last little nuance of

Adam's moods affected them, and they were leaning on her more and more for support.

That was fine—unless Adam *did* intend to end their relationship, in which case how would they cope?

She vowed to take it up with him that night, to tackle him about it and ask him if that was what he intended. She had to know. The waiting was killing her.

And then the phone rang, and the woman from the au pair agency asked to speak to him.

'I'm sorry, he's at work. Can I take a message?'

'Oh, if you would,' the woman said, sounding relieved. 'It's just that the au pair we promised him has broken her leg, skiing, and she won't be able to come for at least six weeks, and I don't have another replacement, not at this time of the year. I'm so sorry. Could you ask him to come back to me if he wants to discuss it further?'

'Sure,' Anna agreed, and cradled the phone.

'Who was it?' Skye asked.

'The au pair agency. Your new au pair's broken her leg and she can't come on Sunday.'

'Yippee!' Danny yelled, leaping up from the table and sending his pasta shapes flying. 'We get to keep you!'

He threw himself at Anna, and she caught him, hugging him automatically.

'We'll see,' she said cautiously. 'I'll have to talk to your father about it.'

'Talk to his father about what?' Adam said from behind her.

'The au pair's not coming, Anna said so, and she's going to stay instead,' Danny said, totally altering the slant on it.

She met Adam's steely eyes frankly. 'It wasn't quite like that,' she began, but he cut her off.

'Really? Perhaps you'd care to explain how it was, then. Children, up to bed, please.'

'But we haven't had pudding!' Jasper said indignantly.

'Take a yoghurt up with you. I want to talk to Anna.'

They trailed off, and she turned to face him, her anger boiling out of control. 'What the hell was all that about?' she demanded in a furious undertone.

'I might ask you the same thing. I come in and my son tells me you've cancelled the au pair and you're staying on in her place—'

'She's broken her leg.'

'So we'll have a different one.'

'There isn't one.'

'How convenient.'

She stepped back, shocked. 'You really think I'd do that? Cancel your au pair and tell the children I'm staying, without discussing it with you?' She wheeled round, too angry with him to stand there, and he came after her, grabbing her arm and turning her to face him.

'Anna, stop. What are you doing?'

'Packing,' she said crisply. 'Let go of my arm.'

'No. You can't go.'

'Watch me.'

'Dammit, talk to me!'

'Why? So you can misinterpret everything I say? Go to hell, Adam.'

He released her. 'You're too late,' he said softly. 'I'm already there.' He turned away. 'For what it's worth, I'm sorry. I didn't mean to jump down your throat. It's just that I'm finding this situation between us more and more difficult, and I was looking forward to getting back to normal.'

Without me, she thought, and her heart nearly stalled.

'We need to talk about this,' she said, but his bleeper went, and moments later he left the house, looking relieved.

Saved by the bell, she thought bitterly, and then the children crept down the stairs, looking ashen.

'Is he angry with us?' Skye asked tensely.

'No, darlings, of course he's not. He's just disappointed that the au pair can't come.'

'He didn't sound dis'pointed,' Danny commented with characteristic bluntness. 'He sounded cross.'

'He's tired,' Anna said, making excuses for him when actually she wanted to string him up and hang him out to dry. 'He'll be all right later. He's working very hard.'

She gave them their pudding, bathed them and put them to bed, then cleared up the kitchen. She'd cooked for herself and Adam, but she had no idea what time he'd be home and, anyway, she wasn't hungry.

She watched television in the sitting room for a while, then checked the children and went up to her room, sitting in the dark and waiting for him. At ten-thirty the phone rang, and she ran down to answer it in his bedroom.

'Anna, it's me. I'm in Theatre. I've had an emergency, and it's going to take longer than I thought. Don't wait up for me, I could be hours. I'll see you tomorrow.'

In fact, he didn't make it home at all, and she took

the children in to the hospital with her at seven next morning.

'Go and find something to do in the playroom,' she told them, and went to speak to the night sister. 'Seen Adam?' she asked.

'Yes, a little while ago. He's in ICU. He's been in Theatre all night, he looks like death warmed up. I told him to go home to bed, but he says he can't. He's got a fracture clinic.'

'Thanks,' she said, and went to find the children. They were happy with the toys, so she left them to it and took over the ward and started on the morning routine.

The taxi driver came as usual and took the children off. Unusually, Jasper was clingy.

'You'll have a lovely time at school,' Anna assured him comfortingly. 'And, anyway, it's Friday. It's the weekend tomorrow—we'll do something nice together, all right?'

'Promise?'

'I promise,' she said fervently, and hoped that Adam did nothing to make her break it.

Adam appeared at eight-thirty for a quick ward round, and he looked awful. Her natural sympathy came to the fore, and she remembered his words the night before when she'd told him to go to hell. 'I'm already there,' he'd said, and today he looked it.

'Why don't you get your registrar to do your fracture clinic so you can rest?' she suggested.

'He already is. We're both doing it. He's no better than me—we were both up all night.'

'I'm sorry.'

He sighed and met her eyes, and his were red-rimmed and bloodshot. 'How are my patients?' he asked wearily.

'All right. Damian's thriving—still in a little pain but much better. Richard's moving better for the physio—I'll get the notes and come round with you, if you like.'

'I can manage,' he said. Taking the notes from her, he went and spoke to each of his patients in turn, checking the charts on the end of the beds, talking to them, making notes.

'Thanks,' he said when he'd finished, handing back the notes. 'And if you get a minute, could you contact the employment agencies and see if you can get a nanny for the evenings next week?'

'We need to talk about this,' she said firmly, but he shook his head.

'There's nothing to say. I can't go on with this. My parents are back on Monday night, they can cover some of the time—perhaps the nights. I just need someone for after school.'

'So get your secretary to ring,' Anna snapped.

'Fine, I will. I just thought you might like to do it as you know what's expected.'

'Or what's needed? They aren't quite the same thing, Adam, as you well know.'

His jaw tensed, and he turned away. 'I can't handle this. I'll see you later.'

'No, you damn well won't,' she said tightly in an undertone. 'One minute you tell me you love me, the next minute you won't talk to me and you're telling me to find a replacement au pair. What the hell is going on?'

He looked back into her eyes, and his face was

etched with lines of pain. 'Don't, Anna. Don't make it harder.'

'Make what harder? Are you telling me it's over? Because, if so, I think you might at least have the decency to do it in private!'

She spun on her heel and walked off, almost running into the treatment room and busying herself with sorting and tidying the sterile supplies. Hot tears spilled over her cheeks, and she dashed them away angrily.

She never cried! She absolutely never cried, at least not about men, and now this man seemed hell bent on tearing her heart into little pieces.

'We'll talk tonight,' he said from the doorway. 'After the children are asleep.'

'Don't force yourself,' she said, her voice clogged with tears.

'Dammit, Anna—'

'Don't "dammit" me,' she said, spinning round and not caring if he saw the tears welling in her eyes and dripping off her chin. 'I'm not a toy, Adam. You can't just pick me up for your amusement and then drop me because it ceases to be convenient.'

'Anna, that's not what it is.'

'What is it, then?'

He sighed and ran his hands through his hair. 'I'll talk to you tonight. I'll come home as soon as I can, OK?'

She nodded, sniffed and turned away. 'Fine.'

He went out, and the swing door swooshed shut behind him, leaving her feeling more alone than she'd ever felt in her life.

Adam felt sick. He was torn, so torn. His children needed stability. They needed something to rely on.

He couldn't let them get attached to every woman he had an affair with, and he would have to be blind not to see how attached they were to Anna.

Not that having affairs was something he did often. She was the first woman since Lyn, and the thought of touching any other woman after Anna was too painful to consider...

He pushed the thought aside and got out of the car, locking it and walking up the path with dread in his heart. He needed her, and yet he didn't see how he could juggle things so he was living two lives and doing either of them justice. He had to get her out of the house, but could they go back to how they were before? Would it be enough?

God knows. Sometimes he felt he needed her more than he needed air, or water, or sleep...

He went in and found Anna in the kitchen, sitting at the table with a cup of tea. She looked awful. She'd been crying, and her eyes were red-rimmed and swollen.

Adam felt like the worst bastard in the world, but he had no choice. He had to protect his children.

He sat down opposite her. 'Anna, I'm sorry,' he said quietly, his voice rough with emotion.

She met his eyes. 'I thought you said you loved me?' she said in a voice overflowing with tears. 'I thought you cared?'

'I do care.' He sighed heavily. 'I *do* love you.'

'Then what's this all about, Adam? I'm not trying to steal your kids' affection, or come between you, or anything like that.'

'I know. I just can't let them get too close to you, Anna.'

'Why not? They get close to the au pairs, and they leave, and they get close to teachers at school, and go on to the next class, and they make friends and then move, and have to learn to deal with it. Why am I any different? What makes me so special that I'm not allowed near them? Am I an undesirable influence or something?'

'Of course you're not,' he protested helplessly. 'Don't be silly.'

'So why? Why, Adam? I love you. You love me. How can that be wrong?'

He closed his ears to her persuasion. He couldn't let her talk him round. It was too important.

'It's not wrong,' he told her quietly. 'I just have to keep my priorities right, and that's going to hurt us both—I know that.' He swallowed hard, trying hard to shift the lump in his throat. 'You have to leave here. I can't go on like this, wanting you, loving you, knowing it's going to end.'

'So are we going back to the way we were? With you coming round whenever you can spare a minute from your hectic schedule to fit in a bit of sexual recreation?'

'That's not how it is.'

'Isn't it? Sometimes it feels like it. But I've got no choice. You know that. I can't turn you away. You need me, and I need you. I don't agree with you, but they aren't my children, so I'll respect your feelings even though I don't think you're right.

'Just do me one small favour,' Anna went on in a voice filled with pain. 'Don't pretend that what's between us is less than it is. Don't turn our love into a secretive, hole-in-the-corner affair. Keep it separate from your life with the children, by all means, but don't pretend I don't exist. I won't be treated like something you're ashamed of.'

'I'm not ashamed of you, or what we have between us,' he told her honestly. 'Do you want to know the truth? I wish I'd never met you. I was happy before, and now I want things I can't have, and I'm ruining your life. I can't give you children, or happy ever after, and you deserve all that and more. I can't give it to you, and I can't keep you hanging on in limbo—we can't go back to how we were.'

She stared at him in silence for a while, then sighed unevenly. 'So that's it, is it? It's all over? Can you just tell me why, Adam? That's all I want. I just want to know why.'

He chased a crumb around on the tabletop. 'You don't know what it was like with Lyn,' he said quietly. 'Every time she had a period, my life was hell. She cried, she ranted, she accused me of cheating her. We tried everything. Nothing worked. Then she seemed to come to terms with it. She told me she was happy to adopt, but all the time it was festering inside her, destroying her.'

He looked up into Anna's wounded eyes. 'It would destroy you, too. Maybe not at first, but eventually. The need to have a child would tear you apart—'

'No.'

'Yes. Trust me, I know. Every time I look at you I hurt because I can't give you a child. It's basic biology, Anna. Survival of the species. Continuation of the human race. It's fundamental and powerful, and unbelievably destructive—and it'll destroy you as surely as it destroyed Lyn.'

'No,' she said firmly. 'It won't, because I'm not like Lyn. I don't want to have just any child. I want to have *your* child. I want to conceive it, and carry it, and give birth to it, and raise it. And I can't. I know that. It hurts, God, yes, it hurts, but it's nothing compared to the thought of losing you.'

Adam's heart contracted at the pain in her carefully controlled voice. He wanted to stop her, to tell her it was all right—but it wasn't.

'Anyway,' she went on, quietly reasoning with him, 'you can give me a child. You can give me three—three beautiful children who I love more than I can say. And they love me, Adam, and they need me.'

'They'll get over you.'

'No. No, they won't. They need me. Skye, especially, needs me. She needs a mother, Adam, and I want to be that mother. She's so scared to love, so afraid it'll be taken away from her again. You can't take me away from her, Adam, I won't let you. She won't survive it.'

'I have to,' he said rawly. 'I can't trust anyone but myself, Anna. I know how I feel.'

'And do you know how *they* feel?' she interrupted. 'Do you know how sad and confused they've been this week while you've been out at the hospital, burying yourself in unnecessary work? They think you're angry with them, Adam.'

Guilt hit him like a sledgehammer. All week he'd been avoiding Anna, trying to distance himself from her so that the break would be less painful, and all he'd done had been to drive the children into her arms—exactly what he'd been striving to avoid.

'I'll talk to them,' he said. 'Explain.' Though God knows how I'll explain, he thought numbly.

His bleeper squawked, and he sighed raggedly and

stood up, reaching for the phone. He spoke to the hospital, then hung up.

'I'm needed in A and E—multiple trauma, child of ten. I'll be back when I can.'

He headed down the hall, grabbing his coat off the end of the banisters. Anna was behind him.

'I'll wait up,' she said. 'We need to finish this conversation.'

'It's finished,' he told her firmly. 'I'm sorry, Anna—more sorry than I can say, but I can't let it go on. I know you believe what you're saying, but I've heard it all before. It won't work. I want you out of our lives, no matter how painful it will be at first.'

'Well, I'll let you tell the children,' she said, her voice clogged with tears again, 'because I can't.'

'I'll tell them,' he said heavily. 'I'll tell them tomorrow.'

'No. Tomorrow I promised Jasper we'd do something. I can't break my promise.'

'I'm afraid you'll have to. I'm sorry. I have to go.'

He went out, closing the door softly behind him. As he got into the car, he could see Anna still standing in the hall, motionless. I'm sorry, my darling, he said silently. I'm sorry...

Anna stood there for a long time, unable to move, unable to breathe. She heard Adam's car start, then the lights swept across the front of the house as he turned and drove away.

She heard a creak on the stairs behind her and turned, her eyes dimly taking in a little figure standing halfway up, near the banister Adam hadn't yet got round to mending.

'Are you going?' Skye asked in a terrified whisper.

She nodded, swallowing hard. 'Yes. Not now, but tomorrow. I'm sorry. He's going to get another nanny for you—'

'But I want you. I love you.'

'Oh, Skye.'

The tears wouldn't be held in check, and she ran to catch the little girl as she flew down the stairs into her arms. 'Darling, I'm sorry. It's just—'

What? What was it? Nothing just. Unjust, perhaps. How could she explain a father's complex motivation to his tiny, terrified child? 'Skye, I love you, too, my darling, but sometimes things don't work out the way we want them to. But we'll still be together sometimes, I promise. You can still see me.'

'How?' Skye asked in a choked little voice.

'You can come and visit me, if your father will let you, and you can phone me and write to me, and I'll write to you, all of you, and I—I only live round the corner, Skye. When you're older you can cycle round to see me, if you still want to, and we can go shopping together and do girl stuff, OK?'

'But you won't be here to tuck me up at night, and au pairs aren't the same. You're like my mum—she used to tuck me up, and then she died, and Lyn did it, and then she went, and now you're going, too.'

'Shh, sweetheart,' Anna whispered, biting back her sobs. 'I'll still be here for you, I promise. I'm not going anywhere. I just won't be living here any more, but I won't be far away, and I'm not going to forget you—I couldn't forget you. Never. I promise.'

'I want you to stay,' Skye said, and sobbed uncontrollably. Her heart almost breaking, Anna scooped her up in her arms and carried the little girl to her room, settling her down on the bed in the crook of her arm.

'Skye, we can't always have what we want, but sometimes things work out for the best. I have a job to do, and I can't really be here all the time. But if I hadn't stayed we wouldn't have become such good friends, would we? And so it's good that I've stayed. I know you're sad I'm going, and I'm sad I'm going, but we'll still be friends. Do you understand?'

'Sort of,' Skye said with a sniff. 'I was sad when my hamster died, but Daddy said think how lucky I was that I had him and he was such a nice hamster. I suppose it's like that, really.'

'Just like that,' Anna said, aching. 'Now, why don't you get into bed and I'll read you a story—all right?'

'OK. And then you can tuck me up.'

'OK.' Anna picked up a book. 'How about this one?'

'Mmm.'

'Right. "Once upon a time there was a big fat caterpillar..."'

'We lost him. Sorry to get you out under false pretences. He arrested before we could stabilise him.'

Adam nodded. 'OK. I'll go home. Thanks, Ryan.'

He went back out to his car and sat for a moment, dreading the coming confrontation with Anna.

She wasn't going to back down without another fight, he was sure, and every word she spoke was like an arrow in his heart. It all made so much sense, if only he could dare to trust her—dare to believe in her.

'Oh, damn,' he muttered, and turned the key, starting the engine. He had to get it over with, no matter how painful. He had to let her move on, give her a chance.

She'd find love with someone else—someone who could give her the child he knew she needed.

'Hell.' He pulled over and blinked hard, pressing his fist to his mouth. This was going to be so hard to do, but he had to do it for her sake.

He dragged in a deep breath, looked over his shoulder and pulled out into the light evening traffic. He wondered if she'd still be standing there in the hall. He half expected to find her there when he came in, but she wasn't.

He closed the door softly and leant back against it, steadying himself. Give me strength, he prayed silently. Help me do the right thing.

He could hear her voice coming from upstairs, and he kicked off his shoes, stripped off his tie and hung his jacket over the banisters, then walked quietly up the stairs. He'd wait for her. She was with Skye, reading a story, and he sat on the top step and listened to her voice. It was enough to send him to sleep. He was so tired—so tired and sad and full of despair. How would they cope without her?

'"And the caterpillar had turned into a beautiful butterfly." There. Isn't that nice?'

'Thank you.'

'My pleasure, darling.'

'Tuck me up.'

'OK. There. All right now?'

'You will see me?'

See her? Adam's brows pleated in a puzzled frown. 'Of course I'll see you. I promised you, Skye.'

'And you'll write to me?'

Oh, lord. Skye knew. How? Had she overheard?

He listened, agonised, to the rest of the painful exchange.

'Yes, I'll write to you, if Daddy will let me, and you can phone me any time you like, all right? I'll always be there for you, Skye, I promise.'

'I love you, Anna.'

'Oh, Skye, I love you, too, darling. Come on, don't cry any more. It'll be all right. Your new nanny will be nice, and your granny and grandpa will be back soon and you can see them.'

'And you'll see me?'

'Yes. I will see you. I promise. Now, go to sleep, darling, or you'll be too tired tomorrow.'

Tears choked Adam. Slowly, soundlessly, he stood and turned towards Skye's door, just in time to see Anna emerge.

She walked through the door, wrapped her arms around her waist and sagged against the wall, tears streaming down her cheeks.

He was a fool—a stupid, deluded fool. Anna was nothing like Lyn. Lyn had never cried for anyone except herself. Anna was breaking her heart because a little girl loved her, and he was tearing them apart. Tearing them all apart, because he was afraid to trust her, to believe in her, to give them all a chance.

'Anna?'

She looked up, her eyes stricken, and he held out his hand.

'Come—talk to me.'

She came, but she didn't take his hand. She kept her arms wrapped round her body, holding herself together as she followed him down the stairs to the sitting room.

He closed the door firmly behind them and turned to her.

'I'm sorry, I was wrong,' he said unevenly. 'I should have trusted you to know your own feelings. I should have had more faith in you. Just now, hearing you talk to Skye—you're right. She loves you, she needs you, and I think you need her, too. And as sure as God made little green apples, I need you, my love.'

'So what happens now?' Anna said, her voice raw with unshed tears. 'Do I stay as the nanny, or do I go back to being the mistress, or what, Adam?'

'Neither. I swore I'd never marry again, but...I love you. You mean more to me than I can begin to understand. You're my life.'

'You say that, but you were going to send me away, Adam,' she said with her usual logic. 'How can I believe you? What if you change your mind again?'

'I won't,' he promised. 'I was only doing it for the children. I thought it was the right thing to do, and I was wrong. I don't even know if in the end I would have been strong enough to let you go.'

He searched her eyes for any sign of forgiveness, but they were expressionless, shimmering with tears. He forced himself to go on. 'I love you. I need you in my life. Marry me, Anna—please? Be my wife. Be their mother. I know I can't give you the child you want, and that will haunt me to the end of my days, but I can give you more love than you'll ever know what to do with. Please?'

He closed his eyes, unable to bear the suspense, and he felt the soft touch of her hand against his face, brushing away the tears. 'Oh, Adam,' she said gently. 'Of course I'll marry you. I love you. I love you all.'

Adam's arms wrapped round her, crushing her

against his chest, and a ragged sob rose in his throat. 'I thought I'd lost you. I thought I'd said too much—that you couldn't forgive me.'

'There was nothing to forgive. You did it all for love.' She tipped her head back and looked up at him, and he brushed the tears from her cheeks with gentle fingers.

'I can't believe I've found you. I've been waiting for you all my life, and I didn't dare to believe in you. I'm such a fool.'

'No, you're just wary,' she said gently. 'It'll be all right, Adam. You'll see. It'll be all right because we've got each other, and that's all that matters. Just dare to believe, my darling. It's all there, waiting for you. You just have to believe in it.'

He took her mouth in a tender, reverent kiss. Sweet relief coursed through him, leaving him trembling in her arms.

And then a little voice behind whispered, 'So are you going to stay?'

Anna turned, and Adam saw Skye standing in the doorway, her eyes filled with a hope she didn't dare trust. Adam knew exactly how she felt.

'Yes,' he said firmly. 'Yes, she's going to stay. She's going to stay for ever.'

He reached out his arms, and gathered Skye and Anna into his embrace. This was real. This was love. This, he could believe in...

*From rugged lawmen and valiant knights to defiant heiresses and spirited frontierswomen, Harlequin Historicals will capture your imagination with their dramatic scope, passion and adventure.*

*Harlequin Historicals . . . they're too good to miss!*

# Medical Romance™

## COMING NEXT MONTH

### #7 DOCTOR ON LOAN by Marion Lennox

When Christie saves Dr. Hugo Tallent's life, he gives her the help she needs to care for the Briman islanders. Soon he loves the Australian island, and Christie, too, but she won't leave—and there are reasons he can't stay….

### #8 A NURSE IN CRISIS by Lilian Darcy

Dr. Marshall Irwin and nurse Aimee Hilliard were head over heels in love with each other! But when she was financially ruined, she couldn't tell Marsh. How could she keep her independence *and* the man she loved?

### #9 MEDIC ON APPROVAL by Laura MacDonald

Dr. Aidan Lennox seems to disapprove of everything about family medicine resident Lindsay Henderson. So why is his approval so important to her? Underneath, she knows that it's far more than a matter of professional pride!

### #10 TOUCHED BY ANGELS by Jennifer Taylor

Meg's healing touch could bring hope to the people of Oncamba, but she despaired of ever getting through to Jack Trent. As the image of his flighty ex-wife, she had enough trouble convincing him she was up to the job at hand….

MEDICALSCNM0301